BROKEN GLASS

By

Dennis Michael

Noble Legacy Publishing

Published by Noble Legacy Publishing
ISBN: 978-1-911761-13-6

Cover design by Noble Legacy Publishing

For my parents – for giving me life.
For my mother – it has been too long in the making, Mum. Thank you for always being by my side, for being my rock.
Dedicated to my two children, Shondrella and Jayden – for always believing in me and telling Dad that he could do it. I love you infinity.

"A disco ball is made from hundreds of pieces of broken glass – yet together, they create something dazzling and full of light. You are not broken. You're a disco ball. Keep shining."

Contents

CHAPTER ONE 1

CHAPTER TWO 6

CHAPTER THREE 11

CHAPTER FOUR 15

CHAPTER FIVE 19

CHAPTER SIX 23

CHAPTER SEVEN 27

CHAPTER EIGHT 31

CHAPTER NINE 36

CHAPTER TEN 40

CHAPTER ELEVEN 46

CHAPTER TWELVE 49

CHAPTER THIRTEEN 53

CHAPTER FOURTEEN 58

CHAPTER FIFTEEN 62

CHAPTER SIXTEEN 66

CHAPTER SEVENTEEN 70

CHAPTER EIGHTEEN 75

CHAPTER NINETEEN 79

CHAPTER TWENTY 84

CHAPTER TWENTY-ONE 89

CHAPTER TWENTY-TWO....................................94

CHAPTER TWENTY-THREE 97

CHAPTER TWENTY-FOUR 103

CHAPTER TWENTY-FIVE 109

CHAPTER TWENTY-SIX 115

CHAPTER TWENTY-SEVEN 120

CHAPTER TWENTY-EIGHT 125

CHAPTER TWENTY-NINE 129

CHAPTER THIRTY 135

CHAPTER THIRTY-ONE 140

CHAPTER THIRTY-TWO 147

CHAPTER THIRTY-THREE 152

CHAPTER THIRTY-FOUR 158

CHAPTER THIRTY-FIVE 163

CHAPTER THIRTY-SIX 169

CHAPTER THIRTY-SEVEN 176

CHAPTER THIRTY-EIGHT 181

CHAPTER THIRTY-NINE 189

CHAPTER FORTY 195

CHAPTER FORTY-ONE 199

CHAPTER FORTY-TWO 208

CHAPTER FORTY-THREE 216

CHAPTER FORTY – FOUR 222

CHAPTER FORTY-FIVE 227

CHAPTER FORTY-SIX 233

CHAPTER FORTY-SEVEN 243

Foreword

There are stories that entertain, and then there are stories that confront you — that hold up a mirror and force you to reckon with life's fragility, unpredictability, and raw truth. Broken Glass is the latter.

When Dennis Michael first shared the premise of this book, it was clear that this wasn't just fiction. It was something lived, felt, and deeply understood. In these pages, he has carved out a narrative that speaks to the complexity of identity, the hidden scars of family, and the haunting power of secrets kept too long.

What makes this novel compelling is not just its twisting plot or sharp character work — though both are masterfully done — but its humanity. Dennis writes with the kind of clarity that comes only from experience. You feel every quiet ache, every moment of confusion and rediscovery. You walk with Joe, not just as a character, but as someone you might have known. Or someone you might have been.

This is a story about brokenness. But more than that, it is about what remains — and what can be rebuilt — after the glass shatters.

It is an honor to share this journey with you.

Introduction

Broken Glass is not just a story, it is a revelation. At its core, this novel explores the fragile, splintered pieces of identity, trauma, and truth, and how they come together to form something greater, something whole.

Told through the eyes of Joe, a man whose entire past unravels in a single conversation with a private investigator, the narrative delves into a world of hidden family legacies, twisted loyalties, and long-buried secrets. As Joe learns he has an identical twin he never knew existed, one shaped by brutality, institutions, and survival, his own life spirals into a series of revelations he could never have prepared for.

Dennis Michael writes with urgency and empathy, blending psychological suspense with emotional depth. Through vivid characters and gripping twists, he invites us to question what it really means to belong, to survive, and to reclaim one's truth.

This is a story of two lives split at birth and shaped by vastly different paths. One of privilege. One of pain. And the storm that brews when their worlds collide.

Prologue

I stare at the folder on the table between us. It's thick, official-looking. My palms sweat as I reach for it, aware of Alex's gaze on me. "Well?" asks Alex. Aren't you going to see what is in the folder? You wanted to see some identification and some credentials, so go right ahead and take a look for yourself.

I reach for the folder and I open it.

There is a picture of Alex on a blue letterhead with the words PRIVATE INVESTIGATOR in bold red text.

I look at Alex, then back at the letterhead. A private investigator? Why would one be asking about my family history? I start to read whatever is written, and I can see that Alex is a self-employed private investigator based on Emely Street in the city, and according to what I can see, he has been a private investigator for the best part of ten years. He is not saying anything as I peruse the document, and when I finish reading, I close the folder shut, sit back in my seat, and cross my arms across my chest, looking at him.

"So, what does this have to do with me?" I ask him.

"Well, now that you have seen who I am, I would like to tell you the real reason that I am here, Joe. And please try not to interrupt me whilst I fill you in on some things that are going to come as a surprise to you, he says as he scoops the folder off the table, picks the briefcase off the floor, and proceeds to place the folder back in the briefcase.

I am now all ears and eager to hear what he has to say.

He places the briefcase back by his feet, places his arms on the table, and I notice that he has not touched his drink. I uncross my arms and also place them on the table, waiting to hear what this private investigator has to tell me. I am no longer hungry for food; the hunger is now in my mind as I am contemplating hearing what has to be this important for a private investigator to be meeting with me.

Alex clears his throat and begins to speak. His words cut through me like daggers. I have a hard time concentrating, and even though he has asked me not to interrupt his narrative, I can't help but ask him to slow down and start again from the beginning.

"Joe, your mother and father are alive and they never perished in a car crash." He starts again. Bolts of lightning are crashing through my mind as I try to comprehend what this man is saying. I am numb with shock! What did he just say? This is insane!! My biological parents are alive and well!? Surely this is a con, a mistake, subterfuge at the highest level! I try to compose myself, but I can hardly concentrate. My breath catches. A cold sweat clings to the back of my neck. Every story I've ever believed about my past begins to crack at the edges. The room spins, and I grip the edge of the table so tightly my fingers ache.

CHAPTER ONE

I was recently arrested for the murder of a man who's been dead for four years. Now I'm in a small, glass-walled room at the magistrate's court, watching time tick by as if any of it makes sense. As I sit here contemplating the next curveball this beloved life might throw at me... I turn my attention to my watch and quickly compare the time with that of the clock tower at the magistrate's court. I'm lucky that my watch wasn't taken off me; pity the same cannot be said of my mobile phone, which has now found a new resting place as so-called evidence at the police station. They should've taken my charger too—my poor phone's probably already dead. Funny thing to be thinking of at this present moment in time, as I haven't properly digested the predicament that I'm in. Suffice to say that, being a psychiatric professional, I have seen my fair share of disputes about what exactly passes as "normal human behaviour", and I can honestly say that the way that I am behaving now is contrary to my normal parameters. Did I kill someone and forget? It's not the kind of thing that one does and forgets about. I close my eyes, trying to recall the past three days...hell, even recalling the past day is proving to be painfully absurd. I don't know how long I've had my eyes closed for, but I'm awoken from my reverie by someone vigorously shaking my right arm.

"You are free to go now," a voice says to me, and I open my eyes to look up at Francis, who's somehow caught up in this madness with me. Francis is from a firm of solicitors, and I cannot understand where the hell he came from, as I certainly didn't hire him simply because my pockets are nowhere near deep enough to hire a brief. This is one of the quagmires that I must contend with as my life unravels in the most spectacular way. Still sitting down, I look at Francis. He places on the floor a black briefcase that he is carrying and is trying to dial a number on his mobile phone, and stupidly, I find myself envying that he still has his phone. He is rocking a dark blue suit with a white shirt complemented by a red tie, and silver cufflinks are visible as he brings his phone to his right ear and starts talking into his phone. He is wearing glasses with round tortoise-shell frames, and he has blue eyes; he has fine features and has the air of a distinguished man who has lent his name to realms of legislature. He turns to face the wall of glass that separates the inside of the room that we are in from the outside world and steps onto the greying carpet with his shiny black shoes and rests his left palm on the glass. I rest my weary eyes on my beige pants and place my hands on my knees, at the same time wondering why the hell I am wearing beige pants, as I don't like beige as a colour. My shoes are not as shiny as his, and my blue socks peeking over my mismatched shoes, I look like a fashion disaster, considering that I am wearing a grey shirt and black jacket.

But no matter; fashion and appearances are the least of my worries. The last time I wore a tie is so long ago that I can hardly remember, and I know for damn sure that I now definitely don't own one. I rummage in my coat pockets to try and locate my keys, and I realise that the good old police have safely kept them, when I suddenly hear loud shouting coming from behind me. I turn around in time to see this young guy trying to swing a punch at an old gentleman in a grey suit; he misses and his momentum propels him forward. He trips on a chair, crashes down, and smacks his head on a wooden table. As he lies in a crumpled heap on the floor, there are shouts as a posse of men in uniform surrounds him, some kneeling in a valiant effort to restrain him while others are trying to usher the intended victim of the swung punch away from the room.

" Let's get out of here," Francis, still on his dog and bone, shouts, grabs his briefcase, and heads toward the door marked OUT. I hastily get to my feet and follow his lead and steal a backward glance at the commotion behind us, where the young would-be assailant has sustained a cut to his temple and there is blood seeping onto the greying carpet. I step into a hallway lined with pictures of old greying men on both sides and Francis steers us into a side room and as he shuts the door behind him, he disconnects his phone call and says, "that was awkward". Awkward does not begin to describe what I am feeling right now after what seems like a roller coaster of surreal events that began when I got a knock on my front door.

The side room that he has ushered me into is sparsely furnished; there is a huge walnut desk bedecked with old magazines that is sitting at the far end of the room, with a black swivel chair right behind it. Two old, scruffy chairs are facing the desk, sitting on the same greying carpet that seems to be everywhere in this building. Funnily enough, I think about the gentleman in the grey suit who almost got decked, the pictures of the old greying men in the hallway, and then the greying carpet and I think to myself – it sure is one hell of a grey day, not to mention the grey shirt that I am sporting. The walls are adorned with old photographs of different people receiving awards of some sort, and as I eye a water cooler to the left, I suddenly feel thirsty and realise that I haven't had anything to eat or drink for quite a while.

Francis places his briefcase on the walnut desk, puts his phone in his pocket, and motions for me to take a pew on one of the scruffy chairs whilst he remains standing. "There seems to be a discrepancy in the sequence of events that is being presented," he starts, and I couldn't agree with him more. He paces the room, telling me my uncle won't be pleased—and that his intervention means things have truly gone sideways. This has got me straight into shock and disbelief. Uncle?" I ask him. "What uncle, and while we are at it, do you mind telling me who you are, how you know me, what the hell is going on, and where the hell you came from??"

Francis turns his blue eyes at me with a look of utter disbelief and says, "Come now, Chris. This is not the time to start playing mind games. The fact that your uncle has seen fit to send me here should not escape your mind as to the severity of this situation. He has now got me really going, as first, my name is not Chris and I have never been known by that name." Excuse me?" I say. "Did you just call me Chris?" I ask him.

"That is one of the things that we have to unravel," he says as he continues trying to wear out the carpet with his pacing. I stand up and face him, and he comes to a halt, giving the greying carpet some temporary respite.

"My name is not Chris," I tell him. *Is this gas lighting? Misidentification? Or am I just losing it?*

This seems to be getting weird now, and I have the feeling that it seems like a case of very mistaken identity.

Francis turns his left wrist and claps his blue eyes on a relatively expensive-looking timepiece, and with a sigh, says, "Chris, things need to get sorted out quickly. I am waiting for Boris to bring the car to the front door, and then we can go and see your uncle, where hopefully we can get more clarity. I feel as if I am stuck in a nightmare that seems to be getting worse by the minute. My name is not Chris, I don't have an uncle, and I am certainly not in the mood to get into a car with a dude named Boris. "There seems to be a massive misunderstanding, and I think you have the wrong client. I haven't killed anyone, and I DO NOT have an uncle. I realized I'm shouting at Francis, whoever the hell he is.

CHAPTER TWO

Where the hell could they be now?" Francis asks himself as he looks at his expensive watch one more time. I can tell that he is a man who is not accustomed to waiting for things like a car to pick him up.

I embark on a mission to wear out the grey carpet.

" By the way, I have your phone and your keys," Francis says in my direction, and he pats the side of his black briefcase. "They gave them to me, since I'm your brief.". I stop wearing the carpet out and say to him, "Can I have my phone and keys?"

"As soon as we get to your uncle's house, then you can have your phone and keys," he replies. He gets up and walks over to the door as if half-expecting someone to walk in at any moment.

I sit down wearily, still puzzled by how things have panned out. What seems to be going on, and why is it happening? I feel as if I have been drugged or as if I am in a nightmarish situation that is weirdly persistent. The door suddenly opens, and two men walk in. They are both bald, and one of them is quite muscular, with bulging biceps easily visible under his white long-sleeved shirt. He wears dark glasses and a flat cap, black jeans with black trainers and to cap it all he has a gun; the butt sticking out from the front of his jeans. I freeze as I clap my eyes on the gun, then notice the other man leaning in to whisper something to Francis, who appears to recoil as if in shock, then turns around to look at me. This man is of a smaller build, short, and is dressed all in black with a flat cap and dark glasses too and the only distinguishing feature from the other man is that he is not concealing a gun, at least not one that I can see. Francis looks in my direction and motions for me to leave the room with him. I am terrified, and I know it's written all over my face as I slowly stand.

As we exit the room, we encounter one of the uniformed men, who I assume is a court bailiff, who had restrained the young guy who had swung the punch. They stop, look at both Francis and me, and ask if everything is ok. As they do so, I look inside the room that we have just come out of and see that the two men must have hidden behind the doors as they are not visible; I can't see them.

Francis assures the bailiff we're fine and tells me to follow him quickly." Wh... what?" I manage to stammer.

" Boris is waiting in the car, so let's go, Chris," Francis says and starts walking, and constantly glancing over his shoulder. I hastily follow him and catch up with him mid-stride as he opens the door to the outside of the building.

" Who...what...who are these people?" I once again stammer as I follow Francis down a short flight of stairs. We go outside and it is a warm sunny day with a slight breeze blowing, the sky is blue and I am glad to be outside in the fresh air, still in a daze as to what is happening to me at this present moment in time. I scan the area that we've just stepped into and I can see the hustle and bustle of life, people going about their daily business. It is lunchtime, and I can see people sitting on a bench across the building, munching on their food and sipping their soft drinks, and again, the hunger pangs hit. Francis comes to a halt at the bottom of the stairs and starts scrutinising the parking area, and a frown creases his brow. He clearly cannot see Boris or the car that is supposed to pick us up and deliver us to "my uncle's" house.

" Funny that," he says more to himself than to me. He looks behind for the two black guys that had come into the room, and they are nowhere to be seen. He furtively starts looking from side to side, reaches into his pocket, and retrieves his mobile phone.

" I don't like the look of this," he mutters and starts dialling, and once again his silver cufflinks are visible as he waits for the connection to be made with whoever he is trying to contact. By now, I'm on autopilot and just going through the motions. I can't see the two men, and I am grateful that the one with the gun is not there. Francis does not appear to be getting any joy from his phone call. He disconnects and dials again...and again. Something's wrong. I can feel it. Francis dials again, but his hands are trembling now. His eyes dart over my shoulder. Then—Suddenly, I hear a shot ring out and Francis drops down to the ground. He is yelling at the top of his voice, "CHRIS, GET ON THE GROUND!"

I am stunned and just stand there looking at Francis on the floor, crawling towards the edge of the stairs.

" CHRIS!!! GET DOWN RIGHT NOW!!" he yells at me, and I dive to the ground and crawl after him as another gunshot rings out.

This is utter madness. Someone is firing a gun in the middle of the day outside the magistrate's court in a busy city!! By this time, Francis and I are hidden at the edge of the stairs, and the crowd that was eating their lunch has quite rightly given it legs in a valiant effort to save their lives and get away from the gunshots, wherever they are coming from. I can hear screams amid the helter-skelter, and I can see people running into cafes, restaurants, and places where they can find safety.

"What the hell is going on??" I manage to ask Francis. I am breathing heavily and sweating profusely. I look at Francis and realise that there is blood coming out of his nose. What the hell?? Francis has been hit!

My heart skips. Francis — the one person who seemed to know what was going on — is bleeding out. This can't be happening. I drop beside him, helpless. "Francis, can you hear me?" I ask him whilst looking over my shoulder at whatever could be happening behind us. Francis can barely speak. He feebly hands me his mobile phone, retrieves a white envelope from within his coat pocket, which he hands to me, then gestures at his briefcase and manages to utter" run Chris" as blood sputters from his mouth.

I look at Francis and shake him by the shoulders. "What are you saying! Who are those people and why would they want to kill you??" Francis seems to be slipping into unconsciousness. He is trying to say something, but the words fail him, and they don't come out right. Once again, I steal a furtive look behind me, and I can hear footsteps slowly descending the stairs. I take one last look at Francis, pick up the briefcase, and leg it down the car park area as fast as my legs can carry me. I dare not look behind as I have no idea what the hell is going on, and if whoever shot Francis will shoot me too. I round the first left corner at the car park, and I don't stop. I carry on running towards the end of a narrow-cobbled street and take a right turn and emerge onto a busy road. I can hear police sirens approaching from my right on the road that I have just joined, and I instinctively slow down.

 If the police see someone carrying a briefcase and running away so fast from a scene where shots have just been fired, there is no doubt what their next course of action will be. I amble towards a pedestrian crossing and wait for the green man like I had been taught all those years ago. And oh my, it sure seems like a lifetime ago when my life was normal. And just like that, I'm running for my life with a stranger's blood on my hands and a briefcase I'm too scared to open.

CHAPTER THREE

The red brick building on St James Street is just around the corner, just as the vendor a few blocks back had said. I look to my left as a car comes careening by, and as soon as there's a break in traffic, I hurry across to the opposite pavement.

I pause to catch my breath and try to make sense of what just happened. Madness is what it seems like. I still cannot come to terms that Francis, whoever he is, has been shot I walk into the building and head to the reception desk, where a blonde woman sits talking on the phone, and she gestures for me to take one of the plush seats next to the desk.

I admire the simplicity of the place: a brown leather sofa to my right, flanked by a book-lined bookcase. A dark mahogany table with roughly six magazines on top is by the side of the plush seats, one of which is now taken by yours truly, and there is a water cooler in the corner. There is a bronze door next to the receptionist's desk, likely the way past her and deeper into the building. As I sit there with the briefcase that Francis had advised me, no, ordered me to take, I wonder what other surprises are waiting behind that bronze door and as my thinking is going into overdrive, a female voice says, "May I help your sir?" and I realise that the blonde woman is done with her phone conversation and was addressing me. I gingerly get up to my feet and casually state that I am here to meet with Mr Atkins.

She asks whether Mr Atkins is expecting me, and I don't know what to say as I have no idea who this Mr Atkins is, I'm just following the instructions from the letter Francis gave me after he was shot, instructions including the opening combination to the briefcase as well as the PIN for his mobile phone implying that should anything happen to one Francis, a white manila envelope inside the briefcase should be handed over to one Mr Atkins at this address, the red brick building, where I am now standing in reception. Every step toward the receptionist felt like I was walking into a trap, but I couldn't ignore Francis's last words. If I didn't follow through, maybe he died for nothing.

I reply that I have explicit instructions to deliver a message to Mr Atkins and offer Francis's credentials.

She looks at the evidence that I have passed her, pauses a beat, and then says, "Ok, Francis, Wait a minute. She presses a button on her huge control console, exchanges a few words with someone, then says that I could go through the bronze door and that someone will meet me.

I walk into a plush office adorned with pictures depicting animals in the wild in Africa, and my eyes lock on a bronzed wildebeest head just to the left of a wooden desk which was neatly spread out with two sets of silver trays containing several layers of yellow paper and behind that desk sits a man who appears to be in his early fifties; kitted out in a red sleeveless shirt with no tie, a clean shaven face with no glasses and the look of amusement can be seen playing in his blue eyes as he takes in the sight of yours truly standing there with my arms by my side.

The office is neatly set, and it is as if everything that is in there is exactly where it is supposed to be. There is a comfortable-looking chair facing the wooden desk, and I am standing right next to it.

"And how may I help you, sir?" the man starts, bringing his hands to rest on the wooden desk as he appraises me without offering me a seat.

"May I sit down?" I ask, and he nods in the affirmative.

I sit in the comfortable-looking chair, all the while keeping my eyes peeled and fixed on the man in front of me.

"Are you Mr Atkins, sir?" I ask and he again nods to indicate that he is indeed Mr Atkins. I start by explaining that I have been given explicit instructions by Francis, who was acting as my brief (I don't want to go into so much detail as I am still trying to figure out what the hell is going on). I state that Francis is now indisposed and that I am delivering his instructions, hence the reason that I am now in the office with the envelope in my hand. I proceed to offer him the white envelope, and he gently places it on the desk, wringing his hands whilst still looking at me.

"You must be Chris," he says, all the time staring me dead in the eye. I explain that there seems to be a case of mistaken identity as my name is not Chris as I have never been known by that name.

Mr Atkins looks at the envelope on the desk, then back at me. He picks the envelope up, turns it around in his hands, before placing it back on the desk.

"So, what do I call you?" he asks, his attention directed towards yours truly.

I am debating whether I should divulge my details to someone that I have just met, as I have no idea what is going on, and I am not sure that I want to give my information out, especially considering what has happened to Francis, what with him getting shot. I shift uneasily in the chair as I contemplate the events that have brought me here thus far.

"You can call me Joe", I say as I rest my hands on the chair's armrests.

"OK Joe", he says. "Do you understand why Francis was in court representing you on behalf of your uncle?".

I don't, and I say that to him, I explain that I don't have an uncle, my family is small, and I know them all.

He picks up the envelope and opens it, and retracts two typed pages, places the empty envelope on the wooden desk, and starts reading. I am feeling uneasy, and I just want to finish what Francis asked me to do and get the hell out of here. My palms are sweating, and I can't shake the image of Francis coughing up blood. What if whoever shot him is watching this place too? Something about this man, this place, makes my skin crawl. And I get the feeling this is only the beginning.

CHAPTER FOUR

He keeps reading, his brow furrowing deeper with every line. I sit in tense silence, watching his face as he reads. I wish that I were elsewhere, and I start thinking about how I had been watching a recorded game of football before all this madness took over. I'm a psychiatric nurse on the last week of a two-week leave. I live a quiet, sedentary life. I start thinking about Scarlett, a co-worker whom I have been seeing for a while and whom I have got lots of love and respect for. Scarlett's a year younger, but we share everything whether its music, theatre, poetry, food, and club nights on our off days. I was planning to meet her tonight and take her for dinner and I am determined that these shenanigans are not going to stop me in anyway.

I live in a one-bedroom flat on the first floor of a four-storey block. I don't know my neighbours. I keep to myself, always have, I don't like mingling a lot with people. The hunger pangs become even more threatening to my stomach now, and I am desperate to get out of here and go home.

I stand up, briefcase in hand, and as I do so, Mr Akins averts his eyes from the pages that he was reading and looks at me.

"Is everything OK?" he asks as he puts the pages on the desk.

"I've done what Francis asked. I should be going now will leave you to it, and it was a pleasure meeting you," I finish and prepare to leave.

"Wait", he says, and he stands up, walks around the desk, and stands facing me, crossing his arms across his chest as he does so.

I can see that he has got black cargo pants on and he is wearing dark leather shoes, which are gleaming in the office light.

He watches me, and I feel the unease tighten in my chest...wondering what could be in the pages that he has just read.

"Where to now, Joe?", he asks nonchalantly.

I don't feel comfortable explaining to this man that I have just met my plans for the day, and I am feeling that he is not entitled to know anything about me as he is a stranger that I have just met and I was doing Francis, whoever he is, a favour.

I start walking out of the office, and he says, "Keep your phone on, I know it's inside that briefcase, we might need to speak soon."

I open the door, walk straight past the blonde secretary, and before long, I find myself walking outside in the glorious sunshine, and the streets are alive with the hustle and bustle of people going about their daily business. I walk along St James Street towards the intersection of Moorland Road hoping to kill, the hunger and get a cold drink. After wolfing down lamb curry, rice, and samosas, the streets buzz with normal life. I grab a lamb curry, more out of habit than hunger. Every bite tastes like cardboard — my mind's still in that office I am ready to go to my flat, have a shower, charge my phone, and start planning for the rest of the day. I look at my watch and I am starting to wonder what exactly happened to Francis, but I brush this thought aside as I debate on whether to hail a taxi or squeeze onto a bus. I reckon that I am too tired to get on the bus and mix with other commuters, so I decide that getting a taxi is the best option.

I turn from Moorland Road and onto Webster Street, hurrying along towards a taxi rank that I have used before, the last time that I had taken Scarlett out for a meal. It takes me about half an hour to get to my flat, and I walk up the stairs to the first floor. I don't trust the ageing lift, and besides, I only live on the first floor. As I turn the corner to approach my flat, I am surprised to see two women standing outside the door to my flat. They don't see me as I approach; they seem to be locked into some heated discussion.

"Excuse me, can I help you?", I ask as I stand next to them outside my flat's door.

They both turn towards me and look at me in horror, as if they had just seen a ghost.

"You... you..." one of the women stammers, her wide eyes locked on me. She is of medium build, wearing a black flowing dress, she has red auburn hair and is wearing a pair of black sandals, and One thing's for sure — I've never seen her before. She gestures towards me, then the flat, she is trying to speak, but she is not making much sense, if any at all for that matter. The other woman is wearing blue jeans and a white tank top and white trainers, she has got her black hair in a ponytail and appears to be of average build. Her piercing ebony eyes stare straight at me, her mouth starts to open to form words, but nothing comes out.

This is one of the most bizarre things that I have ever encountered, and I am at a loss for words. I don't know who they are. But they clearly think they know me — and that terrifies me more than anything else today.

CHAPTER FIVE

"Who are you, and why are you outside my flat?" I ask, staring at the women, confused and a little alarmed.

"You were just here a minute ago in a black suit carrying a holdall and you gave us each some money to state that we haven't seen you," says the red-haired woman, glancing between me, the briefcase, and her friend.

This is getting really weird now, I think to myself. As if the events of this morning starting with the police knocking on my door, me ending up at the magistrate's court, being with Francis, him being shot, me getting instructions from him as he lay in a crumpled heap, and me ending up meeting Mr Atkins!! This is beyond crazy. Now I have two strange women standing outside my flat stating that I was HERE a few minutes ago in a black suit (I don't own a suit for that matter) and saying that I had given them money to say that they had not seen me!! I'm at a loss for words, none of this makes any damn sense.

"Just who are you?", asks blue jeans and white tank top, peering closely at me.

I look at both women standing there, and I feel as if I am back in the nightmare again.

"Please. Just leave me alone — today's already a nightmare," I say as I reach for my keys and unlock the brown door, and go inside my one-bedroom flat. I shut the door, lean against it, and exhale slowly. Am I dreaming? I ask myself as I walk towards the small table in the middle of my small sitting room. I place the briefcase on the table, I take my shoes off and place them on the left side of the floor. My flat's simple, but it works; it has a 50-inch TV which I had fixed on the wall, there is a Sky box underneath it on a glass shelf, and I had Sky TV installed as I love to watch sports and movies in my free time. I have one three-seater and one two-seater black sofas, there is wooden flooring in my sitting room and my table is sitting on a cream and maroon rug that I bought at a flea market a while back. There is a walnut three – tier bookcase filled with different genres of books as I am an avid reader, I aim for two books a month, when work allows. I walk to my small-sized kitchen, which contains a fridge freezer, an oven, a microwave, a white kettle, and the sink is immaculately clean, as I pride myself on keeping my flat clean. I fill the kettle with water and switch it on, then saunter towards the bathroom, where there is a stand–in shower and the toilet. There is one window, and I pull the blind up to allow some natural light in. I wash my hands in the sink, dry them with a purple towel hanging on a rail next to the toilet, and then I make my way to my bedroom.

I have a double bed which is covered in a red satin sheen cover, there are two giant pillows as I like sleeping with a big pillow and on each side of the bed there are two small bookcases with red lamps atop them. My bedroom is not spacious, so there is only room for one single wardrobe. On a corner to the right is a shoe rack. I don't own many shoes as I am a practical man, and I buy things that will serve a purpose. I grab fresh clothes, run through the usual routine — shave, brush, shower.

, and after I have brushed my teeth, shaved, and had a shower, get dressed in comfortable attire suitable for the weather, and then I gingerly walk into the sitting room. I don't even turn my TV on; instead, I peer out through the window, parting the blinds a bit to see if the two women are still there. Sure enough, they are still out there talking to each other. I debate whether I should go outside and get some more information about whatever is going on, but at that moment, a phone starts to ring.

I remember that my phone is inside Francis" briefcase, and I retrieve it. The numbers unknown. Curiosity wins — I answer.

"Hello", I say.

"Is this Joe that I am speaking with?", a male voice at the other end enquires.

"Yes, this is he", I reply. "With whom am I speaking?", I ask.

"You don't know me, but I am calling you as a friend," the voice says. "You can call me Alex, and I know about what has happened to you this morning, and I bet it has been a huge surprise for you," the voice goes on.

"Surprise?!" I bark into the phone. "What the hell is going on, who are you, and can someone explain to me how I got caught up in all this!" I am now shouting with rage.

There is a pause on the other end, as if this Alex, whoever he is, is weighing up his options on what he can tell me or as I am thinking, *lie* to me about.

I am walking in circles around my small table, I sit down on the two–seater sofa, then I stand up again.

"Listen to me carefully," Alex, whoever he is, is saying. "I am not a threat to you, but there are some things that you need to know. You work for Humanities Care, do you not?", he asks.

How the hell, whoever he is, know where I work, and how did he get my number?

"Who are you?!", I shout into the mouthpiece.

"Like I said, I am calling you as a friend, I have no nefarious reasons, and I think that you should meet me, there are some things that you should know about your life and your real family," he answers.

This has now got me thinking. My real family? What could he possibly tell me about my "real" family? It is well documented that I was an only child to my investor father and my mother who was her secretary, and they had died in a road traffic collision when I was a few months old so I had been adopted by a white family. I did not have any relatives, and I was content and happy with the way that I was brought up albeit some tensions at school because I was a black kid growing up in a white family.

CHAPTER SIX

I'd been told all of this when I was twelve, by the family who adopted me, and I had a hard time digesting that my biological parents had died in a car crash. I'd always wondered about my biological parents — what really happened. The story I was told at twelve had gaps. Now this stranger on the phone says he knows the truth? I'd always assumed their marriage broke down after I was born, and that my father had moved away, and that my mother, finding it hard to bring me up by herself, had decided to put me up for adoption. My childhood was filled with very good memories. I had a good education, was always interested in anything to do with academia and writing, and had gone on to university to study psychiatric nursing. I had always thought about tracing my parents when the time was right, though I never told my adoptive family. As I became older, I always had that nagging thought at the back of my mind to find out exactly what had happened for both of them to be killed in a car crash, and now there is this voice, calling himself Alex, on the other end of the line. stating that he had some things to tell me that I should know about my "real" family. This is getting intriguing by the minute, and I have no idea how to respond, so I don't say a word. With the phone still glued to my ear, I walk over to my three–seater and sit down.

"Are you still there?", his voice comes over the phone, and I just sit there, numb, not knowing what to do or say.

"Who are you, really?", I ask in a calm, measured voice, hiding the anxiety crawling under my skin as I think about what he has said about him telling me things about my real family.

"I know that you have had a hard morning and things have quite unravelled in a way that you did not expect", he carries on. "You are at an age where I feel that you should know your family history, and if you are willing to meet me, I can fill you in on a lot that you don't know," he says.

I have always wanted to find out the circumstances surrounding my biological parents" deaths, but had been too scared of what I would find out that I had put this on the back burner to be approached when I felt that the time was right. As far as I was aware, from the information that I had been told since I turned 12 years old, my father was an only child, as was my mother, and there were no known relatives anywhere. That is why when Francis was talking about my "uncle" sending him to represent me did not make any sense in the slightest.

"Can you at least tell me who you are?" I seem to be pleading with this man, calling himself Alex.

"I have information that is very important to you that I feel has been hidden from you, and I don't feel that it is fair to you," he says. "I can send a car to pick you up, and we can meet at a place of your choosing. You can even call Scarlett, tell her where you're going to be and the name of the person that you are meeting, he surmises.

Scarlett!! This man seems to know a hell of a lot about me, and this piques my curiosity as I would never want anything to happen to Scarlett. I realize that I haven't even called her to fill her in on the events leading up to this situation thus far. I make up my mind that I need to find out exactly what is going on, and I have a feeling that my world is about to be turned upside down.

"How can I get hold of you?", I ask the voice calling himself Alex.

"You think about what I have just told you, call Scarlett, and then I will call you back in twenty minutes and you can tell me your decision," he says. "This is to your advantage and you don't have to meet me if you don't want to," he concludes and hangs up the phone.

As I sit there, I am staring at my phone in my hand and I seem lost in a world where images are crashing through my mind, images about the magistrates" court, Francis, the young assailant who had injured himself, the pictures of the greying men, the grey carpet, the two black men with bulging biceps, Francis getting shot and him handing me the briefcase and instructions to reach one Mr Atkins, the two women stating that I had been there dressed in a black suit and giving them money, and now this! It is madness!! I am thinking that one couldn't make this up; it seems too far-fetched and too bizarre. Way too bizarre!!

I decide that, as the adage goes, nothing ventured, nothing gained, as I want to get to the bottom of all this.

I dial Scarlett's number, and after several rings it goes to voicemail. I try a few more times with the same outcome and finally leave her a message, asking her to call me as soon as she gets my message. After another eleven minutes, the phone rings and I am hoping that it's Scarlett.

"Have you come up with a decision?", it's Alex again on the line.

I explain that I have and decide that I could meet him at a restaurant that I sometimes frequent. I picked this place because the staff there know me and it's only a walking distance away from my flat. I state that I will be there in thirty minutes and ask him how I will find him.

"Don't worry, I will come to where you are sitting," he says and then hangs up the phone.

I peer out the blinds at the window again, and I see that there is nobody out there; the two women have left. I hastily put on my blue trainers, a warm black woollen jumper, and a black overcoat. I put my phone in my pocket, then take the briefcase to my bedroom and shove it into the wardrobe between some magazines that are at the bottom of the wardrobe. What the hell are the magazines doing there? Doesn't matter. I feel that I am ready to go and talk to this Alex, whoever he is. I don't even make a brew that I had boiled the kettle for, and I am still hungry but figure out that since I am going to the restaurant, I can get myself something to eat whilst I am there. I retrieve my wallet from a drawer that is beside the right side of my bed, look around my flat, and then exit, locking the door behind me.

CHAPTER SEVEN

I walk slowly, glancing over my shoulder every few steps, half-expecting those two strange women to appear at my door again. But they don't. At the bottom of the stairs, I pause on the street and scan both directions. I don't know who might be watching.

Traffic clogs the road. A traffic warden is arguing with a Chinese man, who's waving frantically at what I assume is his grey Toyota Avensis. A bright yellow parking ticket clings to the windscreen like a badge of shame. I'm grateful I don't drive. Parking around here is a nightmare. I move quickly past them and head for Water Lock Street. At the curb, I wait as cars roar by, their engines rattling my nerves.

Fifteen minutes later, I arrive outside The Regal Elephant Cuisine, my usual spot. I don't go in right away. Instead, I stroll past the large glass windows, scanning the diners inside. I have no idea what this Alex looks like, so the effort is pointless, but I do it anyway. Outside the next building, I stop and lean against the wall, pull out my phone, and pretend to text. All the while, I keep an eye on the restaurant's entrance. I don't know what I'm watching for, but standing still makes me feel like I'm doing something.

After five minutes, I cross the street and step inside.

Soft music plays from overhead, blending with the low murmur of laughter and conversation. The restaurant's warmth hits me right away cosy, familiar, safe. I love this place. The food is always fresh, no GMOs or antibiotic-filled nonsense, and it's served with genuine smiles.

Straight ahead is the bar, where I spot Scot, who's worked here for as long as I've been a regular. I glance around. The place isn't busy. A few patrons linger at the booths in the back private and dimly lit. Scarlett and I have sat back there before. Near the front, a small table by the window catches my eye. It has a perfect view of the street. I make a mental note to take it. I'm still hungry, but meeting this Alex guy has put me off ordering anything yet. First, I need answers.

"Hey! Don't just stand there!" Scot's voice booms from behind the bar. "Come grab a drink, my friend!"

I walk over, and he clasps my hand in a firm shake. "What brings you in at this hour? Not that I'm complaining. And where's that gorgeous girlfriend of yours?" "I'm meeting someone, important business," I say, ordering a soft drink and chatting with him for a minute before I nod toward the table by the window.

"No problem," he says, grabbing my drink. "On the house."

I thank him, despite my protests, and make my way over.

I sit down, eyes fixed on the entrance. Nothing. Still no sign of anyone new coming in. I take out my phone and call Scarlett again. Voicemail. I don't bother leaving another message. I take a slow sip and try not to spiral.

Then, from the corner of my eye, I notice a man approaching. His walk is precise, controlled, like he's rehearsed it. In his left hand, he carries a black briefcase. He stops at my table, meets my eyes, and slides into the seat across from me. Mixed race, curly black hair, brown eyes. He's dressed in a sharp blue suit and white shirt with the top two buttons undone. He sets a phone—probably the newest iPhone—on the table, and places the briefcase by his right foot.

"I'm Alex," he says, reaching across the table for a handshake. I study him before returning the gesture. His grip is firm; he clearly works out. "I'm sorry about everything that's happened to bring you here," he says. "There's a lot I need to tell you."

"Good. Start with why I've been accused of murdering someone I've never even heard of. Why some guy named Francis was in court to represent me and then got shot. And why someone thinks my name is Chris and that I have an uncle!"

My voice rises, sharp and raw. I don't care if I'm causing a scene. But Alex doesn't flinch. He just watches me calmly, like he's calculating how much to tell me—and when. I'm on edge. He might be the one who finally explains this chaos That's overtaken my life.

"First off," he says, "how this was handled was completely wrong. You should never have been dragged from your flat and arrested without knowing a thing. It's an insult." I want to yell at him to stop stalling and get to the point, but I hold back. Instead, I sit there gripping my drink, eyes locked on his.

"What do you know about your biological parents, Joe?" he asks. Seriously? That's where he's going with this?

He said he had answers, and now he's asking questions? I tense up. I barely know this guy, and I'm not about to spill my life story to a stranger. Not that There's much to tell.

Since I was twelve, all I've known is what my adoptive family told me. That my birth parents died in a car crash. That's it.

"I'd like to see some ID or credentials," I say. "Anything that proves who you are—and why you care." Alex nods slightly, picks up the briefcase, and unclicks the locks. He pulls out a black plastic folder and hands it to me. I pause, eyeing him as he shuts the case and places it back by his foot.

"What's in here?" I ask. Before he can answer, Betty, one of the waitresses, walks over with her usual radiant smile. "Would you like anything to drink?" she asks Alex, flashing me a wink.

"Oh right," Alex replies, ordering two cold drinks, one for each of us. Betty leaves, and for a brief moment, I feel grounded. At least someone here knows me. Sees me. I place the folder on the table and stare at it. Then at Alex.

Then back at the folder. I don't open it. He doesn't rush me. We sit there in silence. And with each second that passes, the air between us thickens.

CHAPTER EIGHT

Betty soon comes back with the drinks order, places them on the table, and after telling us to enjoy the cold drinks, she exits and heads to another table.

"Well?", asks Alex. Aren't you going to see what is in the folder? You wanted to see some identification and some credentials, so go right ahead and take a look for yourself.

I reach for the folder and I open it.

There is a picture of Alex on top of a blue headed letterhead with the words PRIVATE INVESTIGATOR in red.

I look at Alex, then back at the letterhead. *Private Investigator?* Why is a private investigator meeting me and asking me about my family history? I begin reading the document, and I can see that Alex is a self-employed private investigator based on Emely Street in the city and according to what I can see, he has been a private investigator for the best part of ten years. He is not saying anything as I peruse the document and when I finish reading, I close the folder shut, sit back in my seat and cross my arms across my chest, staring at him.

"So, what has this got to do with me? I ask him.

"Well, now that you have seen who I am, I would like to tell you the real reason that I am here Joe. And please try not to interrupt me whilst I fill you in on somethings that are going to come as a surprise", he says as he scoops the folder off the table, picks the briefcase off the floor, and place the folder back inside.

I am now all ears and keen as mustard to hear what he has to say.

He puts the briefcase back by his feet and places his arms on the table. I notice that he hasn't touched his drink. I uncross my arms and rest them on the table, bracing myself. I am no longer hungry for food; the hunger is now in my mind whatever this is, it's serious.

Alex clears his throat and begins to speak. The words coming out of his mouth feel like daggers to my heart. I struggle to concentrate. Despite his plea not to interrupt, I can't help myself.

"Slow down. Please, start again, from the beginning."

He nods. "Joe, your mother and father are alive. They never perished in a car crash."

Bolts of lightning crash through my mind. What did he just say? I'm numb with shock. My biological parents are alive? This is madness, surely a mistake, a scam, some kind of cruel trick. My grip tightens on the edge of the table so hard that my fingers start to hurt.

"Steady yourself, Joe. I know this is a lot—it's a normal reaction to something this huge," Alex says, but his voice is muffled. The room is spinning. I feel like I'm falling over a cliff edge with nothing to catch me. Somehow, I regain enough composure to take a sip of my drink and slump back into my seat. Beads of perspiration form across my brow, but I don't bother wiping them away. It still feels unreal. I motion for him to go on.

"Like I said, this is a major shock, but it's time you knew the truth—where you come from and where you fit in. It's only fair you know about your entire life and your family history," Alex says in a calm, measured, and reassuring tone.

"We've kept track of you your entire life," he continues. "On the instruction and guidance of your father. He felt that now, at 21, it was time you were told everything."

Alex begins his narrative.

I was born twenty-one years ago. I was one of identical twins. Our father was heavily involved in politics and ran a lucrative real estate business with my mother. When she was pregnant with my brother and me, they were forced to flee the country they lived in and seek refuge in Europe. That's where my brother and I were born.

They settled in the suburbs of an idyllic European town. Our father stayed low, trying to maintain contact with a few trusted business associates—most of whom were eventually rounded up and detained. He learned that his businesses had been seized, and that he was being hunted. He cut off all communication with his past.

When we were just a few months old, masked men broke into our home and kidnapped our parents. My brother and I were left alone. It was the nanny who alerted the authorities. The police responded, and That's when we were placed into separate foster care.

This is too much. Not only are my birth parents alive, but I also have a brother—an identical twin.

Alex continues. After nearly two years in captivity back in their home country (he spares the detail of how they escaped

Europe), my parents were finally freed. My father disappeared afterward—off the grid completely. Apparently, he had stashed away money in offshore accounts. He used that to wage a silent campaign for justice, channelling everything he had into hunting down those responsible. Vengeance ran deep.

But what mattered to him most was finding us—his sons. It became an obsession. Alex says my father spared no expense, pulling every string and calling every favour to find us.

As I sit there absorbing all of this, my mind drifts back to the life I know. My adoptive dad, Edward, is a commodities trader—one of the kindest, most solid men I know. He is my dad. He and my mum, Sarah, raised me, gave me the best start in life, and never let me down.

They told me my birth parents died in a car crash.

And now this.

It's not that I never wondered. There's always been a quiet curiosity about where I came from. But this? This is seismic. Not only are they alive, they've been keeping tabs on me all this time? And I have a twin?

I glance at Alex. Well-dressed. Controlled. Steady. He doesn't look like a liar. Still, this is going to take time.

My mum lectures at the community college—a job she's loved for years—and I adore her. I stopped living at home during university, choosing halls instead, but I visit at least once a month. We speak often, especially with how exciting things have been between Scarlett and me.

They love her. We're building a future.

And now everything I thought I knew has just been shattered.

CHAPTER NINE

I want to stop him and ask him questions, but I am also so keen to learn everything that he is talking about. I still cannot believe what is coming out of his mouth. Should I be sitting here listening to this stranger whom I have just met, telling me things that appear to be the stuff of make–believe? I am 21 years old, and this is the first time that I have ever heard of an identical twin brother, let alone that my birth parents are alive and well.

As I ponder this, my mind suddenly flashes back to when I found those two strange women standing outside my door. They had been adamant that I had been there a short while ago, dressed in a black suit, and that I had given them money so that if anyone asked, they would say that they had not seen me. What is going on? Could it be... I push that thought aside as I notice that Alex is looking at me, gauging my reaction. I stretch my legs, sit upright, and ask him to continue.

Alex states that eventually my father had managed to find out where I had been fostered and later adopted by the couple who raised me. However, he hadn't been able to find out what had happened to my twin brother; he was still searching to this day. I look at Alex, and a question begins to nag me. I feel compelled to ask, desperate for clarity.

"Do you know my brother's name?" I ask him, every attention riveted on the answer I'm hoping to receive.

"Of course, I do. Being a private investigator, it is easy to know such things using my field resources and the expertise of my team" he replies.

I wait apprehensively, not wanting to rush him.

"Your twin brother's name is Chris," he finishes.

I am at a loss for words. Chris! Francis had called me Chris! I stand up. I don't know what to do next. I place both of my hands on the table surface and stare at Alex, who sits back in his chair, looking up at me. Suddenly, things start clicking into place, the two women who said they had seen me earlier, dressed in a black suit, and had given them money. That wasn't me. It must have been Chris. If we are identical, then they must have mistaken him for me!

I wearily sit back down, feeling drained. This is a day that will live long in my memory. I am eager for Alex to continue, so I say nothing; instead, I lean forward, rest my elbows on the table, and hold my head in my hands.

We sit there in silence for a few minutes, then Alex asks if I am okay and should he continue.

I motion for him to carry on, and he says that my father had tried to get back to Europe with no success. He had somehow managed to regain control of his business through some confidants and, coupled with the millions that he had stashed away in off shore accounts, had built a mansion within a fortress along the coastline. This fortress had become his headquarters, from where he was running his business empire behind astute and highly secure surveillance. Regimes in his home country had come and gone, and my father and mother had kept tabs on my upbringing from afar. They had not let my adoptive parents know that they were aware of my whereabouts. Apparently, I had been watched most of the time by a team secretly hired by my father. This sounds like a plot from a movie to me, it seems so surreal.

"If my parents know where I am, how come they have never contacted me or bothered to come and see me?" I ask Alex.

Alex shrugs, and just as he's about to answer, I see two dark cars screech to a halt outside the restaurant. I have a clear view of the street outside. I watch as two men rush out of the first car and one man from the second. They are all dressed in black. Alex notices the surprise on my face, quickly turns to look outside, and sees what I'm seeing. He grabs his briefcase and hands it to me.

"Joe, take this and make your way out of here! Use the kitchen and don't stop until you're far away. Don't go back to your flat!" He hands me a folded piece of paper and hastens me to get going.

I cannot believe this is happening again. From the corner of my eye, I see one of the men talking to a waiter at the entrance. I take the briefcase and the folded paper and head straight to the back of the restaurant, where I know the kitchen is located. "Hey

"Hey Joe!" a voice booms from the left. It's Scot asking if I'd like another drink.

I ignore him and push through into the kitchen. I need to find sanctuary somewhere safe in case someone is waiting at the back exit. I don't even know where this kind of thinking is coming from.

As I make my way inside, the first thing that hits me is the frenzied energy of the kitchen. The heat from the stoves, grills, and ovens is intense. The clanging of pots and pans and the sizzle of sautéing ingredients create a chaotic symphony. But amidst this chaos, There's an undeniable rhythm and purpose. Each cook moves with robotic efficiency, chopping, slicing, and dicing at lightning speed. Their movements are so fluid and precise, it's hard to believe they're under such pressure to deliver high-quality dishes for the diners waiting outside.

I slip into a cubicle labelled "Staff" that overlooks the entire kitchen through a clear window and shut the door behind me. I deduce this is a short break room for staff to rest while remaining on standby. I sit on a wooden chair and tuck the briefcase under a spotless metal table to my right, which is set against a cream-colored wall.

I can observe the kitchen just by raising my head through the window. The head chef, a towering man with a thick beard and stern expression, commands the kitchen with quiet authority. He moves from station to station, tasting sauces and adjusting seasoning, his palate discerning even the most minor deficiencies. It's clear he's a master of his craft, and he demands nothing less than excellence from his team.

CHAPTER TEN

The waiters move in and out of the kitchen, arms loaded with plates of food that look like works of art. The presentation is impeccable—vibrant colours and textures that are as pleasing to the eye as they must be to the palate. Each dish appears to be a symphony of flavours and aromas, meticulously prepared with a level of care and attention that only comes from masterful culinary hands. I know this not just because I'm hiding in this small staff room, but because this is my favourite restaurant. I've had countless dinners here. Suddenly, I feel the pangs of hunger and wish I had ordered something before Alex arrived.

What is happening to me today? I whisper to myself.

It feels like I've been through hell, and I haven't come back yet—the nightmare keeps unfolding. I don't know how long I can stay here. Sooner or later, someone is bound to walk in and find me. I glance at my watch—twenty-five minutes. That should be enough time for those men to have left. I wonder if Alex is okay. Why did he give me the briefcase and that folded piece of paper? Why did he insist I shouldn't return to my flat?

My thoughts drift to Scarlett. She still hasn't called back, and I hope she's alright.

Slowly, I get to my feet. Everyone in the kitchen seems engrossed in their tasks. I slip out quietly and head towards a sign marked "Waste Disposal".

I hurry toward the door, guessing it's where the kitchen disposes of its waste, and find myself in a backyard cluttered with metal containers, vats of oil, a forklift truck, several metal trolleys, and two white vans parked side by side. I walk toward what I assume is the main entrance. The sun is still shining. It's surreal. All this chaos in my life, and the world outside keeps spinning like nothing's changed. I need to get far away from this restaurant, so I start walking quickly, falling in step behind a group of Japanese tourists chattering and snapping pictures. They seem so carefree. I wish I felt the same.

I make a mental note to call Scarlett again and, as I pass an arcade, I hear music drifting from within. I follow the sound inside. The arcade is like a mini shopping mall; cafes, restaurants, bookstores, even a pharmacy. A cabaret bar seems to be the source of the music. I notice a small open seating area shared by the adjacent coffee shop, with a few people enjoying their drinks and conversations. I take a seat.

A waiter approaches, and I order a lemon green tea. As I wait, I unfold the piece of paper Alex gave me. It contains the combination to unlock the briefcase.

The tea arrives. I thank the waiter, who moves on to another table. With a glance around, I place the briefcase on the table and gently open it using the combination.

What I see inside takes my breath away: bundles of banknotes, a mobile phone, a Hilton Hotel key card with a room number, and neatly folded paperwork. The Hilton. One of the best hotels in the city. That says something about Alex.

I close the briefcase and set it on my lap. Sipping the tea, I pull out my phone and try Scarlett again. Voicemail. Again.

I know now, I won't be going back to my flat. So I might as well head to the Hilton and see what other surprises are waiting for me. I'm exhausted and starving. A warm meal and a bed sound like heaven.

I pay for the tea and start walking. The Hilton is about ten minutes away.

It still feels unreal, all of this happening in just a few hours. It feels like I've been living inside this nightmare for weeks. I walk along Lyell Street, swallowed into the crowds of people going about their day. I glance over my shoulder every now and then, hyperaware. A new instinct is developing, situational awareness I never had before.

Suddenly, a thought strikes me: why don't I just go to the police and tell them Suddenly, a thought strikes me: why don't I just go to the police and tell them everything? Let them handle it. I could go back to living a normal life.

But then I remember—they already arrested me. At the crack of dawn. They know something's going on. Still, I decide to first check into the Hilton and then consider heading to the police.

As I approach the hotel, I see two sleek black limousines parked out front. The concierge is doing his job well, smiling and welcoming guests. He turns to me.

"Good afternoon, sir. Welcome to the Hilton."

I nod politely and walk through the revolving doors into the grand lobby.

The Hilton lobby is a picture of indulgence. Organic swirls of foliage rise up through the space. It's clean, efficient, yet somehow comforting. A calming transition from the chaos of outside to the serenity of inside. Soft, pastel lighting washes over everything. I feel the day's tension start to melt away.

I don't need to check in, I've got Alex's room key and the number. I find the elevators, scan the key card, and ride silently to the sixth floor. Soft music plays in the background, and before I know it, the doors open with a whisper.

I follow the signage to room 605, insert the key card, and the door clicks open.

Soft lighting greets me. I step inside, close the door behind me, and take in the room.

The floor is covered in soft lilac, with transparent sections revealing glass beneath. A king-size bed dominates the centre. Across from it, a sleek fireplace supports a massive TV screen. To my left, a table is set for six; an opulent fruit bowl at its centre atop a gold-and-silver cloth. A plush mahogany chair with red velvet upholstery waits by the side.

I notice another door. A bathroom. I turn on the light.

It's stunning. Spa-sized bathtub. Stand-in shower. Scented candles. A silver-and-gold toilet cistern. Floor-to-ceiling cabinets. Marble bidet. It's luxury beyond anything I've ever seen.

I walk back into the room, still holding the briefcase. I place it on a spotless marble desk beside a silver telephone. On the side table is a gold-plated room service menu.

Nearby, what should be a minibar is actually a full-sized fridge humming quietly.

I open it.

Inside: milk, cheese, mozzarella, margarine, jam, pickled onions, caviar. I chuckle. Caviar in a fridge. I remember from my waiting days" caviar should never be frozen. Unopened, it can last in a fridge for twenty days, but once opened, it's best within three.

There are five bottles of Veuve Clicquot champagne. That, too, brings back memories from hospitality gigs. Veuve Clicquot is top-tier, a global symbol of luxury.

There's white wine, soft drinks, and beers like Carlsberg and Budweiser. The freezer is stocked with everything from fish fillets to chicken nuggets.

None of it appeals to me. I want real food.

I pick up the menu, settle into the mahogany chair, and skim the options. A five-course dinner grabs my eye.

Course one: "Holy Grain Sourdough" with Lancaster Cheese Custard, Brown Onion Tea, and Cheshire Estate Marmite Butter. Marmite? Nope.

Course two: Aged Sirloin Beef Tartare with Brussels sprouts, Miyo Mayonnaise, and smoked tongue. Smoked tongue?! No thanks.

Alternative: Red Prawn, Fermented Green Chilli, Lime, Cucumber. Pass.

Course three: Creedy Carver Duck Breast, Fried Bun, Hen of the Woods Mushroom, and Braised Carrot in Hoi Sin Sauce. Hmm... tempting, but not today.

Grilled Halibut: Fermented Celeriac, Celery Leaf Oil, Welsh Mussels. Nope.

Course four: Gorgonzola Cheesecake with Pear, Celery, Rehydrated Grape (what even is that?) and Gingerbread. Who eats like this?

Dessert: Chocolate Cremeux with Sesame Tuile, Chocolate Shortbread, and Sesame Praline Ice Cream.

I drop the menu and pick up the phone, hitting the room service button. A voice answers smoothly.

"What would you like delivered to Room 605, sir?"

I scratch my head and sigh.

"Please may I have a sirloin steak—no tongue, thank you—medium rare, with fries, a salad, and onion rings, if possible."

CHAPTER ELEVEN

The food is delivered to the room in less than an hour, and within that time, I have gone through all the contents of the briefcase. Alex Symonds works on Emely Street; he is the owner of a private investigation company that appears to have no name. There's an address and several landline telephone numbers, but beyond that, there isn't much else to discern. I've counted the money in the briefcase, which totals a staggering ten thousand, four hundred and sixty pounds. Who walks around with that much money in a briefcase and then casually gives it away?

As I enjoy my meal, I find myself thinking more and more about Alex and what may have happened to him. It's becoming clear that someone out there is actively trying to stop anyone attempting to help me make sense of this chaos. Alex gave me a jolt from the blue, and now, he's the one person I want to see again, perhaps even more than Scarlett. Speaking of Scarlett, I pull my phone out and try calling her again, but this time it doesn't even ring—it goes straight to voicemail. That sends a shiver through me. It's her day off. We were supposed to meet this evening. I have a gnawing feeling that something isn't right.

After finishing my meal and washing it down with a glass of cranberry juice from the fridge, I place the used utensils on the silver trolley and wash my hands. I glance at my phone—33% battery. I don't have a charger, but then I spot a small side drawer by the bed. Sitting on top is a sleek wireless charging pad. I walk over, place my phone on it, and immediately an instant message flashes up: OPTIMAL CHARGING IN PROGRESS.

I start thinking about my next move, but a knock interrupts my thoughts. The server is back, wheeling away the trolley. He asks if I enjoyed the meal, and I nod. Once he exits, I sit on the bed. It's impossibly comfortable, and despite everything, I feel like I could sleep like a baby. But I don't have time. Scarlett isn't answering, and I need to check on her.

I look at the phone again, it's now 87% charged. I blink. Is this how the wealthy live? Super-fast everything? Regardless, I'm grateful. I walk over to the massive wardrobe at the end of the room, slide open the glass doors, and am greeted by a walk-in closet bursting with elegant clothing. Suits in every shade: black, grey, navy, teal, red. Shirts with nautical stripes, rows of neatly folded T-shirts and shorts. Everything appears tailored to someone my size.

The shoes; dozens of them—are all size nine. There are ties, jackets, jumpers, even designer underwear. I open one drawer and find gold cufflinks; another has expensive-looking watches. I shut the last drawer quickly when I discover the underwear—none of this is mine.

There's a full-length mirror. I study myself. My clothes are fine; I don't need to change. Besides, these Aren't mine to wear. A sharp beep from the charger pulls my attention. My phone is now fully charged. I grab my coat, place the electronic key card in my wallet, and tuck it inside my jacket. Then I head out.

The lobby is buzzing. A Chinese tour group is clustered together, their guide looking harried as he reads names off a list. I weave through them and step outside, scanning the street for a taxi. I spot one, flag it down, and climb into the back.

Just as I'm about to shut the door, it's yanked open.

A bald, muscular man is suddenly there. He's dressed in a tailored black suit that clings to him like a second skin, and he has the kind of build that only comes from lifting heavy things for hours every day.

"Are we okay back there?" the taxi driver calls out. "The meter's on, just so you know." He's clearly uncomfortable, eyeing the man through the rear-view mirror.

"Get out," the bald man says, grabbing my left arm.

"Who are you?" I manage.

"I'm not going to tell you again," he says. His voice is calm, eerily so. It's not loud, but it scrapes along my nerves like sandpaper. There's menace in it, coiled like a snake ready to strike. It's the kind of voice that doesn't need volume to be terrifying.

He starts pulling me, pressure building on my arm. I stumble out onto the pavement. He shuts the taxi door gently, raps on the side of the vehicle, and the driver, clearly wanting no part of this, takes off into traffic without a word.

CHAPTER TWELVE

The man gently propels me away from the pavement and onto the left side of a tall building a block away from the Hilton, where a grey, nondescript Mercedes Benz is parked. I can see that someone is at the wheel and the engine is running. He opens the back left door and ushers me inside— and this time, I'm really worried. Am I being kidnapped from a busy street at five o'clock in the evening in front of a thousand witnesses?! Mr. Bald Head squeezes in after me, shuts the door, and the car takes off.

"Excuse me!" I shout. "Do you mind telling me what the hell is going on here?! I'm going to call the police!" I continue, reaching into my pocket and retrieving my phone, which is instantly wrestled out of my hand by Mr. Bald Head.

"What the hell do you think you're doing? I'm a citizen, and I demand to be let out of this car!" I shout as the car drives along.

I valiantly try to unlock the right-hand back door, but it won't budge. I look around the car—it is a Mercedes alright, but There's nothing remarkable to note. I can't see the driver, as There's a partition dividing the front and back, much like there was in the taxi. Only difference: this one is blacked out, with no way to see ahead. Mr. Bald Head doesn't even look at me; he's staring intently forward as the car manoeuvres through evening rush hour traffic. I glance outside, but I can't see anything, the windows are blacked out from the inside. I imagine all the people hurrying to their various destinations after a hard day at work, some heading home, others to restaurants, pubs, gyms, and here I am, in the back of a black Mercedes with a muscular, bald-headed guy who pulled me from a taxi, being driven to God knows where.

"Do you have a name?" I shout, looking at him. He doesn't utter a word. He doesn't even turn his head to acknowledge me just keeps staring straight ahead.

I take a closer look at him. Suddenly, a realisation hits me, this is one of the men who were at the magistrate's court when Francis was shot!

I am suddenly paralysed with fear. Not this, I say to myself. I slide as far away from the man as possible and start wondering where I'm being taken and what will happen to me. This is the day from hell. I can't believe I'm going through this. Sheer and utter madness. Lunacy.

I decide to speak again, because if I don't figure out What's going on, I might not make it out of this.

"Why did you have to shoot that man this morning?" I ask, not expecting an answer.

He once again completely ignores me.

"Is he dead? Do you know what happened to him, and where he is right now?" Yours truly keeps up with the questioning. Still no response—no acknowledgement that I'm even sitting next to him.

"Where am I being taken?" I press on like a dog with a bone.

I eye him more closely, wondering if I should make a bold, brave—albeit stupid—move and rush him. But it would be futile. The man is nearly twice my size. I give up on that foolish idea and start contemplating the meaning of all this.

First, I get arrested on a murder charge. Francis shows up and gets me out, apparently sent by my uncle. He gets shot. I don't know if he's alive. I meet Mr. Akins. I meet Alex, who tells me the most incredible story, one that could change anyone's life. He hands me a briefcase full of money. I go to the Hilton. Scarlett won't answer my calls. On my way to find her, I get bundled into the back seat of this Mercedes Benz. You couldn't make it up. It sounds like the stuff of fiction.

Before long, the car slows to a stop. There's a brief lull, then it lurches forward again for a few minutes before coming to a full halt.

My door opens from the outside. I stay seated. A short man in a black beanie hat leans in and asks me to step out. I reluctantly do, and as I rise, I look around and see we've arrived at some kind of modern two-storey house.

There's a lush green lawn and the front is clean and simple. The front door is wooden and white. Several cars are parked under a carport. Apart from the short man who opened the door and the other two men, no one else is visible. The driver makes a beeline for the entrance, opens the door, and the other two walk me toward it.

As I step inside, the world explodes.

A sudden burst of gunfire erupts from somewhere I can't see. Mr. Bald Head takes a shot to the temple and crashes to the ground. The driver turns toward the gunshots—and is blown off his feet, slammed into the wall in a hail of bullets. I instinctively dive to the floor as the short man tries to shut the door. But he's picked off by several shots, parts of his skull splattering across the entrance.

Mayhem!

I crawl into the house on my stomach, using my elbows and knees. I roll onto my back and try to kick the door shut, but it won't budge—the short man's body is wedged against it. I hear footsteps approaching from outside. From my prone position, I scan the room for somewhere to hide. Getting away from whoever's coming is paramount.

There's no time to admire the opulence of the hallway or the décor. I get up into a crouch and half-sprint, half-walk toward a door immediately to my right. Just as I reach it, a voice booms from behind.

"Stop, Joe."

The voice is commanding. I freeze, straighten up, and raise my hands, my back still turned.

"You can turn around now," the voice continues.

I slowly, deliberately turn, hands still high.

There's a man holding a gun in his right hand. He's black, quite slim, about six feet tall and roughly 190 pounds. He's wearing a black cap that casts a shadow over his face, making him appear menacing. He's also wearing black leather gloves.

Menacing? Hell, he just shot three people!

CHAPTER THIRTEEN

He takes a measured stride towards me and tells me to lower my hands which I gladly do. I dare not take my eyes off him as he holsters his gun, takes his gloves off and comes to a halt right in front of me. At that exact moment, I hear my phone starting to ring; I know the ring tone that I have programmed so that I will know whenever Scarlett calls me, and I quickly steal a glance at the dead bald man on the floor where the ringing tone is emanating from as he had wrestled my phone off me in the car. The man in front of me doesn't budge. He simply stands there as if appraising me and I don't know what to say. At this moment in time, I am completely at a loss for words and I am on the verge of going crazy.

The man then slowly and methodically turns around, dons on some blue rubber gloves from a hold – all that is behind his back and starts towards the bodies lying on the entrance to the house. He pulls all the busies inside and then shuts the door, reaches into the bald man's pockets and retrieves the phone which has stopped ringing by now.

"Is this your phone?" he asks me, holding the phone in his right hand.

I now take a closer look at him and see that he is clean shaven and has brown eyes and a scar on the left side of his cheek. He is dressed all in black with black boots.

"Yes," I manage to say.

He puts the phone in his pocket and then motions for me to follow him as he starts walking away from the entrance and inside the house proper. We walk into a spacious living room which is bright with blue walls and salmon flooring. In the centre of the room is a large blue carpet, on which are placed two sofas, a coffee table, and several stools. There are book shelves containing many books and decorations including a plant and a clock. I look around and notice a fireplace with some pictures on top, there are four windows and two of them have got lovely violet curtains. There is a medium – sized TV on a stand by the corner and as I am taking all this in, the man motions for me to sit down on one of the sofas. I gladly oblige and as I do so he pulls out a phone from his hold – all and dials a number. I don't hear the conversation as I am busy scanning the rest of the room; there are two doors leading away from the living room on opposite sides. The man speaks on the phone for a few minutes then hangs up, puts the phone in his pocket and turns around to face me.

"My name is irrelevant to you", he starts. He does not offer a greeting and he appears all business.

"All you have to know is that these men have kidnapped you and you were in mortal danger and I am here to make sure that that did not happen. There is someone who is going to explain all that you are going through and then you can do whatever you feel is right with your life".

He is so matter – of fact and straight to the point.

"There is a car that is just around the corner and I am to take you away from here but understand that I have no nefarious reasons and I mean you no harm" the man concludes and it doesn't appear as if there is going to be any further conversation. He walks towards the door and in about ten minutes, time that I spend just fidgeting and wishing that I wasn't here with those three bodies by the entrance. There is the sound of two vehicles pulling up outside the house and the man motions for me to join him. He is a man of very little words, I surmise.

He opens the door and there are four black men there; they are also all dressed in black with black caps and black sunglasses as well as black boots but no one has got any weaponry that I can discern. Three of them appear to be carrying what appears to be a crime scene cleaning kit – I have watched crime documentaries so I am aware of how clean ups are carried out, in a way. The three men file into the living room and not one of them looks in my direction. The fourth man has a quick chat with the shooter who once again motions for me to follow him outside, where he leads me to a black Toyota Avensis with blacked out windows. The fourth man gets behind the wheel of the car and the shooter and I get in the back and without further ado the car takes off to goodness knows where. We drive in silence for the best part of forty-five minutes and I decide that I am not going to ask any more questions, I decide to let whatever is happening play itself out. I suddenly feel very tired, maybe it is the resulting meal that I have had at the Hilton making me feel sleepy. I shut my eyes for a few minutes and after a while I feel the car come to a stop. I can hear noise and the sounds of multiple engines as well as raised voices and the honking of cars.

"Let's get out" the shooter says to me and he exits the car and I follow suit.

We are in what appears to be an underground car park. As I look around, I realise that this is what I have been doing a lot during the course of today – going in places that I have never been before and looking around, taking stock of my surroundings. The car park is like a small jungle with untamed beasts – except that the beasts are cars parked haphazardly in every which way and it appears to be a chaotic mess of metal and noise, with cars jutting out at odd angles and drivers honking their horns with frustration as they are trying to exit the car park; it seems that there is broken down car that is obstructing everyone's progress. The air is thick with the scent of exhaust fumes mixing with the overpowering smell of oil and the sound of a car alarm blaring and engines revving is creating a symphony of noises that is assaulting my ears and rattling my brain. The driver starts walking and leads the way and I am in the middle as the shooter falls in line behind me. We meander our way through cars, past the maddening cacophony that is taking place and the driver approaches a bank of elevators, reaches out and pushes a button.

There are two elevators and one of the elevator doors slides open and we file inside, the driver selects the sixth-floor button. It feels like déjà vu; at the Hilton I had gone to the sixth floor and now here we are riding to another sixth floor. No matter, I think to myself, let me see what is in store of this sixth floor and take it from there. We ride slowly in silence, the two men do not say a word to each other and once on the sixth floor, the shooter gets out first, scans the corridor outside and motions for me to follow him. The driver doesn't exit and as the elevator door closes shut, the man starts walking to the left and I fall in step next to him.

The corridor is just that – a simple corridor. There is shiny wooden flooring and there are a few doors adjacent to each other as we walk past them. The man stands behind a brown wooden door, knocks twice and waits. Before the door is opened, he hands me my phone, not uttering a single word to me. I notice that there is a ring doorbell on the door, and I know that these ring door bells have helped with solving a few crimes where criminals had broken into some homes so I am aware that they are very useful. I know that the ring chime connects to all ring video door bells and security cameras so that one can hear real – time notifications. After a minute, the door swings open, and standing behind the door is Alex, the private investigator.

CHAPTER FOURTEEN

"Welcome, Joe," says Alex, extending his right hand in greeting while gently pulling me inside, his left hand resting lightly on my back as he guides me into the sanctum—whatever this place is.

I'm taken aback, in a sort of mini-shock. What is Alex doing here? I wonder. He walks me through what appears to be a hallway and into a small living room, where he offers me a seat and takes one himself. I notice the shooter didn't follow us in, he must've stayed outside the door or left altogether. I don't dwell much on Mr. No-Name. Instead, I focus on this strange new environment, which feels slightly more comfortable only because I've met Alex before, and I'm eager to hear what he has to say.

Alex walks over to a cabinet along the left-hand wall, where a tray holds an assortment of drinks, alcoholic beverages, soft drinks, and water. For a brief moment, I feel like downing a few shots of something strong, but when Alex asks what I'd like, I settle for a glass of water. He pours himself a generous measure of Macallan single malt Scotch whisky, and I can tell this is a man accustomed to a high standard of living.

"Just give me a moment, Joe," he says, placing his drink on a doily on the table before stepping through a door to the right.

As I sip my water, I glance around. The space isn't as grand as the Hilton suite from earlier, but it's tastefully decorated. A cream three-seater sofa sits on a white carpet, in front of an expensive-looking glass table. A silver stool sits nearby, and a reclining chair is placed near the door Alex just entered. Apart from a silver dining table with four chairs, there isn't much else of note. The walls are painted white, and a large window near the dining table is dressed with cream blinds and silver-plated curtains.

I take another sip of water and suddenly remember Scarlett had tried to call me. I quickly pull out my phone and, sure enough, her name is on the missed call screen.

I tap her number, she's on speed dial, but it goes straight to voicemail. I check for any text or voice messages. Nothing. I try again. Same result.

Just then, Alex walks back into the room carrying a small brown leather case and a blue binder thick with paperwork. He sits at the dining table and gestures for me to join him. He places the binder in front of him.

"Joe, this is the story of your life," he says calmly, "and I'm going to tell it to you without interruptions. After that, you can decide what you want to do. I'll also go over the money I handed to you in the briefcase, but understand this: the money isn't mine. It's rightfully yours."

I take another sip of water, fix my eyes on Alex, and brace myself. I decide not to interrupt, just listen and let it all unfold.

Alex begins again: I was born 21 years ago, part of an identical twin set to parents who loved their new-born sons dearly. As he explained earlier in the restaurant, my father was a wealthy businessman, running a successful real estate company with my mother. He was also involved in politics.

When the political situation in their home country grew dangerous, they fled to Europe seeking refuge. That's where my brother and I were born.

They settled in a peaceful town, and my father tried to stay connected with his old business associates, many of whom had been arrested or disappeared. Eventually, he learned his business had been taken over and that he was being hunted. To protect us, he cut ties with everyone from his past.

When we were just a few months old, masked men broke into our home, kidnapped our parents, and left us behind. It was the nanny who alerted the police. My brother and I were eventually placed with different foster families.

Alex, still untouched drink by his side, reads from his notes in the blue binder, maintaining sharp focus. I listen intently. I'd heard some of this before, but now I'm hungry for details.

After the abduction, nothing was ever heard about our parents again. My brother—Chris, and I were split up. The family who took me in kept me permanently. Chris, however, was moved from one foster home to another. I want to ask why, but I hold my tongue, trusting that Alex will explain in due time.

He tells me my upbringing was stable. I attended good schools and had a decent childhood. He doesn't linger on abstract details. Somehow, my father eventually gained his freedom and went into hiding. From afar, he tracked down my foster parents and arranged for people he trusted to keep an eye on me. Unfortunately, he was never able to locate Chris, despite years of searching.

My father couldn't return to Europe—why, I don't know, but he remained in hiding while I finished school, went to college, and graduated from university with an honours degree. I can't complain about my life, but it's strange hearing all this now—strange knowing my parents are alive and that I have an identical twin brother out there.

Alex explains that five years ago, he was hired to oversee my transition into adulthood. My father, he says, had something important to pass on to his sons and wanted to ensure I was protected and prepared.

I'm itching to ask what my father's business was called, but I hold back. I've come this far; I can wait a little longer.

I sip my water again. Alex does the same with his whisky, still scanning his documents with careful attention. I stretch my legs, straighten my arms, and rest my elbows on the table. Then, as Alex pulls out a gold pen from the brown leather case, I stand and ask where the bathroom is.

Without looking up from his paperwork, he gestures toward the door he had entered earlier. I head that way, retrieving my phone from my pocket. As I enter, I find myself in a small library lined with bookshelves and scattered magazines. To the left, I see a white door, I assume That's the bathroom. I dial Scarlett's number again.

CHAPTER FIFTEEN

Sure enough, it is a bathroom, a celebration of white and chrome, with a sprig of lavender in a vase that feels surprisingly soothing to the senses. It's clearly a place for washing, for nurturing one's sanity through the comfort of warm water and aromatic soaps, which are neatly arranged next to the chrome porcelain bathtub, itself beside the toilet and bidet.

But I'm distracted now. I'm really starting to worry about Scarlett, her phone keeps going to voicemail, and I'm suddenly struck by a dreadful thought. I finish my business, rinse my hands quickly, and dry them with a crisp paper towel, which I drop into a chrome bin by the sink.

As I walk back toward the living room, one thought grips me: *What if Scarlett has been taken by the same group of men who brought me here?*

I hurry to Alex, who is no longer reading from the binder but instead swirling his whisky glass slowly in his right hand.

"Alex," I say urgently. "Do you know if something's happened to Scarlett? I've been trying to reach her with no success! Her phone was ringing at first, then it started going straight to voicemail. I have a missed call from her, it came in while all these shenanigans were going on, and I'm really worried now. If you know something, please tell me."

Alex stops swirling his drink and looks up at me.

"I don't think anything's happened to Scarlett," he says calmly.

"And how do you know that? How are you so sure?" I sit down, my eyes fixed on him.

"If anything had happened to her, I would know instantly, Joe," he says, placing his glass carefully on a napkin on the table.

"How do you mean?" I ask, then immediately realize who I'm talking to, a private investigator who's been tracking my life for the last five years.

"Rest assured, we'll go and meet her when we're finished here," Alex says, returning to the binder and his paperwork.

He continues, explaining that my father managed to keep running his business without ever appearing in public, relying on a tight circle of loyal associates. According to Alex, my father's wealth is vast, and since he only has two sons, and I'm the one he's been able to track, he wishes to meet me privately to share something significant.

"What about Chris?" I ask, my voice more tentative now. "And why was I framed for murder and dragged into court this morning? Who the hell is Francis?"

Alex crosses his arms, leans back in his chair, and fixes his gaze on me.

He explains that since being hired five years ago, his firm has uncovered a few things about Chris. While they couldn't trace every family he was passed between, they learned enough to know that Chris had become a feared figure in certain circles, a man with a ruthless streak and a tendency toward violence. He was rarely seen in daylight, and his whereabouts were largely unknown. He kept a tight-knit group of loyal cronies.

Alex tells me Chris had a deeply troubled upbringing. Being moved from one foster home to another did him no favours. He eventually fell in with the wrong people and ended up in youth detention, followed by multiple stints in prison, for drug dealing, burglary, attempted murder, and attempted rape.

Jesus, I think. *My twin brother? Is he sure about this?*

Alex continues: the police have been looking for Chris for years. At some point, someone noticed our resemblance and tipped them off. I'd apparently been placed under surveillance, but investigators were baffled when I was seen going to work every day, living a completely normal, quiet life. I wasn't involved in anything criminal.

But Chris was wanted for the murder of a man from four years ago, after new evidence came to light. A police sketch, based on a witness statement, ended up being a dead ringer for me.

Alex flips through a few pages, runs his finger down a line, and then explains that identical—or monozygotic (MZ)— twins occur when a single fertilized egg splits in two after conception.

He adds that this split typically happens around the time the fertilized egg becomes implanted in the womb. These twins share 100% of their genetic material—including the same blood type.

I sit there, stunned, thinking: *Damn. I'm learning more today than I have in years, and the day's not even over.*

Not only are my parents alive, but my father is a wealthy man who has quietly watched over me my entire life. I have an identical twin brother I never knew existed, one who's been through hell, has a rap sheet a mile long, and is now wanted for murder. And because of our identical DNA, the police thought I was him.

CHAPTER SIXTEEN

I am waiting to hear where Francis and the so-called uncle fit in.

I must be crazy! Three men have been shot dead, and I'm sitting here trying to work out where this uncle fits into it all. Shouldn't we be calling the police? Why am I acting like this is all normal, like this chaos is somehow right up my alley? I should be in pieces by now!

I look hard at Alex, and he looks right back at me.

He can't tell what I'm thinking, and he doesn't ask.

I'm still trying to make sense of the situation I'm in. Before he can say anything, I blurt out, "Who were those men, and why did they kidnap me and bring me here?"

Alex doesn't look away. He closes the blue binder, clears his throat, and begins to speak.

He explains that the so-called uncle is actually a man named Marcus. Marcus had known about Chris and me. He was aware of our father's wealth and had been working behind the scenes, orchestrating Chris's descent into criminality, all in pursuit of that wealth, by any means necessary.

"Who is he? And where is he?" I ask, trying to sound a little more menacing than I feel.

Alex swivels to his left, uncrosses his legs, and places his open palms on his thighs, facing upward. I've seen this before in psychiatric training: a non-threatening gesture, meant to signal openness and trust. I'm suddenly hyper-aware of his body language, reading everything while trying to kick my tired brain into gear. I need a plan. Fast.

Alex says Marcus lives in the southeast of the city, in a gated mansion with 24/7 security. He used to be an associate of my father and rarely ever leaves his home.

I ask, "If he wanted my father's wealth and knew about Chris, why didn't he take Chris, who'd gone off the radar, and use him to access that money?"

Alex explains that Chris had been too damaged. Years of polysubstance abuse had left him psychotic. He was only useful to Marcus as muscle, to do his dirty work.

Apparently, Marcus had also tried to keep tabs on me once rumours started circulating about where I was. There had been a clause—a proviso—that stated when Chris and I turned 21, we would inherit large sums of money, *provided both of us were of sound health and mind.*

That's why my father had tightened security around me, security I wasn't even aware of. He hadn't known Chris was being manipulated into illegal activities.

Alex goes on: Chris had botched a major drug deal. Someone described him to the authorities. That triggered a reopened cold case involving a murder from four years ago. A police sketch based on a witness description looked exactly like me.

As the police began surveillance, on me, Alex's team noticed almost immediately.

Chris had disappeared after the failed deal, which had cost Marcus a lot of money. No one could find him. Rumours spread that he'd fled the country, but Marcus vowed to hunt him down.

Then Marcus got word that police had someone under surveillance who looked like Chris. When he heard "Chris" had been arrested—meaning *me*—he summoned Francis, his lawyer, to handle the situation personally. He instructed him to pull out all the stops and bring "Chris" to him. That's why Francis kept telling me everything would be explained once we got to my "uncle's" house.

It all starts to make a weird kind of warped sense now.

I glance at the time and remember I'm supposed to meet Scarlett within the hour. As if reading my mind, Alex says he'll take me to her soon.

"So if Francis was taking me to this "uncle," why was he shot?" I ask. "Who were those men, including the one who pulled me out of the taxi when I was heading to meet Scarlett?"

I walk over to the cabinet with the water pitcher and refill my glass. Alex joins me, topping up his Macallan. We stand there, holding our drinks. I take a large gulp of water, waiting for him to answer.

He walks back to the dining table. I follow, and we both sit.

"Those men were part of the failed drug deal," he says. "They had no intention of taking "Chris" to any uncle. They lured Francis into a false sense of security. Their plan was to kidnap "Chris," bring him here, and then demand a ransom for his release."

That doesn't make any sense to me. *If Marcus was furious at Chris, why would he pay money to get him back?* Or… would he?

Alex continues, explaining that the men thought I was Chris but had doubts. Chris was far more muscular than me and didn't dress anything like I did.

That sets off alarm bells in my head. A bright red flag is now waving before my eyes.

CHAPTER SEVENTEEN

If those men were meant to bring Chris here, then how did the blue binder with all this paperwork, that Alex got from the room that looked like a library, get here? Who really was Alex?

I don't say this aloud. He can see the confusion in my eyes but says nothing.

"And what about Mr. Atkins?" I ask him.

"Mr. Atkins is nothing to do with you. That, we assume, is between Francis and himself, some form of insurance policy. Don't forget Francis really thought you were Chris, as he'd never seen you or Chris before. And just so you can breathe easier, he wasn't severely injured. He's okay," he finishes.

I drain the rest of my water, then ask him what the plan, the course of action, is.

He explains that, for now, the plan is to keep me safe. The shooter was still outside.

I ask why he doesn't just inform the police, remembering I had apparently been bailed from court that morning. Surely, the police will come looking for me.

Alex reassures me that that confusing matter has already been taken care of and that There's nothing to worry about. He adds that his team is actively looking for Chris and, given Chris" deteriorating mental state, he's confident they'll find him sooner rather than later.

As I sit here going over everything That's happened today, Alex appears calm. Too calm. There's something bothering me, and I'm eager to dig into it. There's this persistent, nagging doubt in the back of my mind, something more to Alex than he's letting on.

"What are my parents" names?" I ask, staring him dead in the eye.

"Alfred," comes the reply. "Your father's name is Alfred, and your mother's name is Kathleen."

Alfred and Kathleen? Those are the names of my biological parents. I say this silently to myself. I interlock my fingers and stare at the floor.

Alfred and Kathleen. Hmm.

Suddenly, I want to know everything about them. Their lives, whether I have extended family—so many thoughts are racing through my mind.

I glance at the time and tell Alex it's time to go meet Scarlett. He packs everything away, stands, and walks to the front door while I remain seated. I hear him talking to the shooter. After a few minutes, he returns and states that we can go outside, where a black BMW 3 Series is waiting.

Sure, the 3 Series has some of BMW" s best engines, top-tier powertrain calibration, cutting-edge technology, incredible build quality, and probably the best performance. I remember this because, back at university, one of my friends had been obsessed with German cars. And to be fair, the 3 Series is among the very best sports sedans in the world. I've always wished I owned one, but right now, I feel overwhelmed by everything That's going on.

I sit in the passenger seat as Alex gets behind the wheel. I don't know what he's said to the shooter, and we drive off into the dusk slowly enveloping the city. The Car's interior looks sharp and solid. I recall that early models in this generation had a plain dashboard, but this facelifted version features the so-called curved display, a vast sweep of screens, one for the driver and another to control the infotainment system. I know it's familiar from other BMWs, but it gives this 3 Series undeniable wow factor. There's a smattering of physical controls lower down on the dashboard and centre console, but most of the Car's features are controlled through the screen.

We hit the busy roads and sit in silence. I don't ask any questions. I trust that Alex knows where Scarlett is, and I can't wait to see her. Still, questions are coursing through my mind. What do my parents look like? Where is Chris? To me, none of this makes much sense.

If Chris is really suffering from a mental health disorder, then how was he outside my flat in broad daylight, dressed in a suit and handing money to those two women? Is Alex keeping something from me?

I'm pragmatic. I don't take things at face value, something drilled into me during my three years at university. We were always taught: if someone says something is, question it. Ask for evidence. Ensure There's something solid to back it up.

So far, I've taken Alex at his word. But the one compelling moment I can't let go of is how those two women reacted outside my flat. They were astonished at seeing me. That was genuine. They couldn't have faked that. I know how to read human behaviour, and there was no mistaking their sincerity.

I just wish I had questioned them more.

I look out the window as we meander through the city. After about forty-five minutes, we pull up to a well-lit street lined with posh vehicles and a few pedestrians going about their evening. I check my watch, six p.m. Scarlett and I were supposed to have dinner at the Regal Elephant at seven, so despite everything That's happened, we're still on time.

The street we've pulled into is unfamiliar. I know Scarlett doesn't live in this part of the city, but at this point, nothing surprises me.

"Where are we, and why are we here?" I ask Alex, casting a sideways glance as he kills the engine and turns off the lights.

He lets out a deep sigh, looks at me, and explains that he had Scarlett brought here, where it's safe. He wasn't sure if anyone might try to get to her to lure me out.

I don't respond. I turn to look out the windshield. The street sign to the left reads: Roseberry Street. I've never been here before. It doesn't look rough, in fact, it looks calm, serene, and oddly comforting.

Alex gestures for me to get out. I exit from the passenger side. He does the same from the driver's side, bends down to pick up his things, including a black holdall, walks around to the boot, pops it open, deposits his stuff, and shuts it. Straightening up, he blows out his cheeks and motions for me to walk with him.

Roseberry Street appears to be a long, quiet block lined with modern houses and a mix of vehicles. The pavements are clean, clearly well-maintained, and I can tell this is an affluent area. The streetlights haven't come on yet, and the soft glow of early evening casts a warm hue over everything.

We walk to what looks like a newly built house with a white door, sandwiched between two smaller homes. Alex knocks.

After a few seconds, the door opens. A tall black man stands before us—around six feet, roughly two hundred pounds, with a black beanie and clear reading glasses. He's wearing a grey short-sleeved t-shirt stretched over visibly worked-out biceps, black cargo pants, and black trainers. Without a word, he gestures for us to enter with his right hand while keeping his left on the doorknob.

CHAPTER EIGHTEEN

The house is welcoming from the open door to the wide hallway. Upon the walls are a series of photographs, and the floor appears to be old-fashioned, an earthy blend of subterranean browns. The walls, painted in the greens of summer gardens, meet an intrepid white baseload, creating a vivid contrast. Alex steps in first, and I follow as the man shuts the door behind us.

Alex turns, gestures toward the man, and says, "This is Steve."

"Steve, you don't need me to tell you who this is," Alex adds.

"Welcome, Joe," Steve says, offering his hand for a handshake.

His voice is low and smooth, his smile easy and discerning. I like him already.

"Nice to meet you, Steve," I reply, shaking his hand.

I follow Alex into what appears to be a living room. It's nothing out of the ordinary, just a comfortable-looking space. Three sofas line two of the four walls. One wall has a TV and a cabinet filled with DVDs and photos. The opposite wall holds a computer table, with CDs stacked neatly beside it. In the centre lies a rectangular rug with swirly patterns, and atop that sits a medium-sized coffee table.

This room might be ordinary, but it holds something extraordinary for me: Scarlett is somewhere in this house. I'm slightly disappointed she's not already in this room.

Steve slips through a door beside the TV, and Alex and I sit on one of the sofas. A wave of fatigue hits me, but I'm holding on, waiting with bated breath.

The door opens again, Scarlett walks through.

I leap up and rush to her. We embrace tightly. In this moment, nothing else matters. Her presence soothes my mind like a balm.

At five foot six, Scarlett is nearly as tall as me. Her brown skin glows, and her long, black micro-braids cascade down her back. She has her mother's features: The Nubian nose, deep ebony skin, wispy eyelashes, plump coral lips, and brows that furrow inward, as if constantly assessing the world.

Her blue silk brocade dress enhances her natural beauty, hugging her crescent waist. She's lithe and elegant. Her brown eyes mesmerize me. They're intense, smouldering, eyes that see too much. When she smiles, it's radiant. No makeup, she doesn't need any. She's the most beautiful woman I've ever seen.

We walk back to the sofa hand in hand. She sits beside me, close, not letting go. I smell the perfume I gave her last week, floral, soft, like a melody. It stirs something deep, like a song of peace and home.

She's wearing pink, fluffy flip-flops and leans in, resting her head on my shoulder.

"See, I told you nothing happened to her," Alex says.

I glance at him, then look back at Scarlett, puzzled. She smiles again, gently squeezing my hand.

"I met Alex today," she says, reading my mind. Her voice is like a lullaby.

I glance at Alex, then check my watch.

"After we got wind that you were being set up, arrested as part of a ruse to take you to Marcus, I had to make sure Scarlett was safe," Alex says. "I instructed the team to keep her phone off in case Marcus's people could trace it."

He looks at Scarlett warmly. "But true love wins out. She turned it on to contact you."

"Thanks for keeping her safe," I say. "But we've got plans tonight. We really need to get going."

Alex looks thoughtful, then stands and walks over to the computer table. He perches on it, facing us.

"Joe, you can't go back to your flat," he says. "That suite at the Hilton is still yours, for as long as it takes. Hopefully, not long. I know you're on annual leave, and if things go well, you may never need to return to work."

His voice is authoritative. Scarlett and I stay quiet, listening.

"The money in the briefcase is yours," he continues. "I have your number, I know where to reach you, but I doubt I'll need to. We've got eyes on you, you're safe. Don't return to your flat. Everything important has been moved to the Hilton. The briefcase Francis gave you is secure. And the black leather wallet, it's now in your room's safe."

He hands me a small leather-bound wallet resembling a menu. I take it with my left hand.

"This should all be over soon. We'll finish the debrief tomorrow. You've had enough for today. Enjoy your evening. Feel free to tell Scarlett everything, she knows some, not all. You'll be driven to the Hilton. From there, the night is yours."

He steps toward the door Steve and Scarlett had used earlier.

I turn to Scarlett and hold her tightly. My world has flipped upside down, and I'm struggling to process it. I gently cradle her face and look into her feline eyes, luminous and knowing. We stay like that, locked in our own quiet world.

Then Steve returns.

"Car's ready," he says.

We stand together. Scarlett follows me, still holding my hand.

Outside, the BMW idles at the curb. A black man sits behind the wheel.

Steve opens the car door. "Have a good night."

We climb in, and he closes the door, then disappears back inside. The car pulls away into the soft, quiet evening.

CHAPTER NINETEEN

We hold hands as we are driven to the Hilton.

"I have so much to tell you that you're going to freak out," I say to her, squeezing her left hand. She rests her head on my left shoulder, and it feels so comfortable, like I don't have a care in the world. I wish time would pause and let us stay here forever.

She tilts her head and looks up at me with that smile that always makes me melt. I still can't believe how lucky I am that Scarlett is my girlfriend. I must be the luckiest guy in the world. She snuggles closer, squeezes my hand back, and we ride in silence until we arrive at the Hilton.

The same concierge from earlier greets us as we approach the lobby. The driver pulls away in the BMW as we step inside. Scarlett is visibly mesmerised by the Hilton's opulence, the foliage in the lobby rises in organic swirls, calming to both eye and soul. The atmosphere retains its clean efficiency and warmth, softly lit as though sunshine were cast in gentle pastel hues.

I lead her over to the elevators and we ride up to the sixth floor. Once inside room 605, we fall into a wildness of kissing and hugging and more kissing before finally collapsing on the bed to catch our breath.

"This is an example in luxury," Scarlett says with a soft giggle. "What have you done to deserve all this? Alex said he had surprising news about your parents, but he didn't tell me the full story. Did they win the lottery or something and now someone's after you for ransom?"

She giggles again, propping herself up on one elbow with her head resting in her palm. She traces a line on my face with a finger while kicking off her pink fluffy flip-flops. I take off my trainers, place both her flip-flops and my shoes neatly on an expensive-looking shoe rack, and turn back to admire her.

"Really, Joe," she says, laughing.

I don't understand. I stand there staring at this beautiful woman and realise she's my entire world.

"Really what? Did I do something wrong?" I ask as I return to the bed.

"Firstly, you're on annual leave. Secondly, you're in the Hilton. And all you can think to do is arrange shoes? Can you just switch off for one minute and stop taking life so seriously?" she teases, play-punching me in the chest.

"Aw, that hurt," I fake a wince, pulling her close. We start kissing again.

Eventually, we both lie back. "Have you eaten today?" I ask, looking into her beautiful eyes.

"Actually, not really. I've been too worried about you. Alex told me something happened at the magistrate's court but said you'd fill me in. Why don't we stay in, order room service, and just catch up tonight? You must be exhausted."

She rests her head on my chest, and I begin stroking her hair.

That sounds perfect, even if I had promised her dinner out. What better place for dinner than the Hilton? I already know the menu's top-tier.

I sit up and tell her the food is excellent, explaining I'd ordered from room service earlier. Taking her hand, I walk her to the gold-plated menu on the side table next to the fridge-freezer.

"Have a look at this," I say, letting her browse while I open the fridge. "Help yourself," I offer, grabbing a bottle of mineral water.

"Good luck with the tongue bit," I tease, tickling her before heading to the wardrobe with the glass doors. I slide them open and am surprised to find women's clothes, expensive-looking ones, lined up alongside several stylish shoes. I open drawers that previously held cufflinks and watches, now filled with colourful women's underwear.

On the left-hand side, I notice a glass door I hadn't seen before. There's a small button to the right. I press it gently. With a soft hum, the door slides open, revealing what looks like a private office. A medium-sized mahogany desk stands at its centre, elegant yet bare save for a silver rotary dial telephone. A leather chair sits behind it, its cushion seemingly untouched.

Tasteful artwork hangs on the walls, but otherwise the room feels stark, almost reverent. In the corner next to the chair is a large safe. I walk over to it and read: *De Raat Domestic Safe DS 404E*. I reach into my pocket, retrieve the leather-bound wallet Alex gave me, and find the safe combination.

I decide to wait until Scarlett finishes ordering so we can open it together. There's not much else in this room, so I quietly exit, press the button again, and with a soft hum, the door closes behind me.

Back in the main room, Scarlett is still scanning the menu, now holding a glass of white wine in her right hand.

"Any luck?" I ask, sitting beside her and placing my arm around her waist.

She looks deep in thought. Knowing her, she's already decided what to order—she's meticulous about food.

I place our order and, while we wait, I begin recounting my day: the police knocking on my door, my arrest, the station, then the magistrate's court, Francis, the two guys, the gunshots—when the food arrives. It's delicious, and she, as always, chose perfectly. She's quickly becoming my other half.

When I ask about her day, she tells me to finish my story first. Her table manners are impeccable.

We enjoy our meal and dessert. Two servers come to clear the dishes, again asking how the food was. Afterwards, we settle on the huge, comfy king-size bed, side by side. We don't turn the TV on. We simply hold hands. Scarlett uses the silver lilac bedcover to tuck in both our feet. I continue telling her about my surreal day.

I mention Mr. Atkins, the two women outside my flat. She's visibly shocked, but I tell her There's more. I go on about the phone call from Alex, the meeting at the Regal Elephant, sneaking out through the kitchen, the briefcase full of money, and how I got kidnapped, and how the kidnappers were shot and killed.

It feels like I'm narrating a Hollywood film. Scarlett stops me now and then, asking questions and prompting me to clarify certain parts.

CHAPTER TWENTY

"Brace yourself, sweetheart," I tell her, about to share the most shocking part of the day.

She stiffens, snuggling even closer. She places her glass of white wine on the bedside cabinet, atop a white doily, eyes locked on me, eager for what I'll say next.

I close my eyes and let out a soft sigh, then begin in a flat monotone, recounting everything Alex told me. I ask her not to interrupt, but when I mention that my biological parents are alive and that I have an identical twin brother, she sits upright and stares at me.

"What did you just say?" she asks, mouth slightly open.

I repeat what Alex told me, still trying to wrap my own mind around it. Scarlett has always known I was adopted, I told her early on, and she's always been my rock. She also knows I had a great childhood, nothing to complain about, but I'd always wondered about the car crash that supposedly killed my birth parents. To hear they might still be alive, that I have a twin, it's a sledgehammer of a revelation.

She doesn't speak. She just pulls me into a tight hug, as if afraid to let go.

"What if it's true?" I ask her, holding her even closer.

She has tears in her eyes and blinks them away, reaching for a tissue from the man-sized box on the cabinet.

She's clearly in shock, and who could blame her? She keeps looking at me, as if waiting for my reaction.

I take a breath, then continue: Alex said my twin has a troubled past, criminal charges, addiction, mental health issues. We sit in silence, still holding hands, lying back and staring at the ceiling.

"You said those two women outside your flat saw you earlier, dressed in a black suit, and that you paid them to deny seeing you if asked," she says slowly. "But if you live there, wouldn't they assume it was you anyway? So why pay them off, unless that really was your twin?" She grips my hand tighter.

I've been wondering the same thing. If Alex is telling the truth, and the women's comments seem to back it up, then yes, I have a twin brother named Chris, wanted for murder, and being hunted by someone named Marcus over a botched drug deal.

I'm just glad I've told Scarlett. We lie in silence, letting the weight of the news settle. My mind is racing, I need proof. Pictures, videos, anything. Something real.

Twenty minutes pass. I can feel her warm breathing on my chest, calm, steady, and I savour that peace.

Eventually, she gets up to use the bathroom. When she returns, I tell her we need to open the safe.

"More surprises, I guess," she says, taking my hand as we step into the walk–in wardrobe. I press the button; the glass door hums open. Scarlett freezes, staring at the hidden mini–office.

"Who has a mini–office in a Hilton walk–in wardrobe?" she asks.

I shrug and lead her to the safe. I retrieve the small leather-bound wallet, remove a folded gold slip of paper, and read off a series of numbers, the safe's combination. I enter them. There's a click. The door swings open.

Inside is Alex's briefcase, and next to it, a leather–bound binder, about the same size. Scarlett and I exchange glances. I lift the briefcase, place it on the mahogany desk, and unlock it. Scarlett gasps at the neatly stacked bundles of money still inside.

Next, I pick up the binder. No clasp, just two zippers running the perimeter. I slowly unzip them.

Inside, I find a thick plastic loose–leaf wallet. From unit, I remember what these usually held, notes, assignments, reading material. But these... these are different. The first wallet holds a stack of green papers, each stamped with bold gold lettering, the name of a company I've never heard of.

Scarlett reaches for another sheet, same company name, same gold lettering. My curiosity spikes. I suggest we take the binder into the bedroom and read it properly. One thing catches my eye: the name "Alfred" at the bottom of the paper I'm holding.

I close the safe, snap the briefcase shut and leave it on the desk. I carry the binder, and Scarlett scans her page as we return to the bedroom. The door slides shut behind us. We sit on the bed. I place the binder on the dining table.

From what I'm reading, the company is called CODENEINIS INVESTMENTS — headquartered in Nairobi, Kenya. That rings a bell, my adoptive parents once told me that my birth parents were originally from Kenya.

I'd done my own research: Kenya, the "Pride of Africa," had always intrigued me. English and Swahili were the main languages. Nairobi, the "City in the Sun." I'd always wanted to visit.

But now, that curiosity burns with urgency.

The document says the founder and chairman is Alfred Keynudhia.

My heart skips a beat.

Is this my father? My biological father?

According to Alex, yes, this is him. My father. His surname.

The company is listed as a private limited entity, distinct from its shareholders. It's a legal person, in essence. It deals in real estate and manufacturing. No financial statements, just general info.

Scarlett looks up from her page.

"It says here that Mr. Keynudhia owns the company, and that all its assets are to be transferred to his heirs upon them turning twenty-one," she says, locking eyes with me. "Do you know what this might be implying?"

I stare back, heart pounding. We've only scratched the surface.

Alex's words echo in my head: *if everything goes according to plan, you may never need to work again.*

This day keeps getting stranger. Suddenly, I feel exhausted. I don't want to look at any more papers. I just want to rest. Scarlett senses this and squeezes my hand.

"Are you okay?" she asks.

No. Not really. I feel overwhelmed.

"I think we should rest, get some sleep, pick this up tomorrow," I say, voice low.

She nods, hands me the page she was holding. I tuck both sheets back into the plastic wallet and zip the binder shut, leaving it on the table.

I mention the women's clothes in the wardrobe, probably Alex's doing, and joke that if they're not to her taste, she can't blame me.

She laughs lightly. I stretch my arms and she starts browsing the wardrobe.

Even though it's only ten, we decide to get ready for bed. I change into white shorts and a vest from the wardrobe's neatly arranged contents, all my clothes from the flat are here too.

Like everything else today, it feels surreal.

CHAPTER TWENTY-ONE

I take my socks off and put them in a laundry basket at the end of the wardrobe doors, then walk over and sit on the bed. I glance at the TV mounted on the wall but feel no desire to watch anything, which is strange because I usually enjoy the ten o'clock news. Tonight, though, I'm just not in the mood. I pat the two giant pillows into place, pull the covers back, and just as I'm about to slide in, I remember, I haven't brushed my teeth.

I walk over to the bathroom. Scarlett is still choosing her nightwear, so I leave her to it. The bathroom is still bathed in luxury, the scented candles exuding a soft, pleasant aroma. I open the floor-to-ceiling double cabinet and find an impressive array of soaps, deodorants, shaving foams, creams, toothpastes, and toothbrushes. I choose a blue toothbrush and some toothpaste, head to the sink, and rapidly brush my teeth.

As I walk back into the bedroom, I see that Scarlett has changed—and I stop, caught in awe. If the black heavens of night could be transformed into silk, the nightgown she is wearing would be the result. It's a silky black midi-dress with velvet spaghetti straps, hugging her form like a second skin. The gown seems like an evolution of the classic satin night slip, and all the better for it, I'm thinking.

"You look like you're about to faint," she teases, sashaying toward me with that magnanimous smile I love so much.

"You're beautiful. Just... beautiful," I say, clasping her right hand and pulling her gently toward me. I kiss her softly on the lips. She laughs and playfully prods me in the ribs.

"Get in there," she says, pointing to the bed as she untangles herself. "I'll quickly brush my teeth and join you." She heads off to the bathroom.

I climb under the warm covers, lie back, and mull over what we've just read. Investment company owned by Alfred Keynudhia. Hm.

Right now, the weight of the day is catching up to me, and I'm so glad Scarlett is here. She soon joins me, switching off the main lights. The room glows softly, lit only by the warm light of the side lamps on our bedside tables. We talk about what we plan to do tomorrow, cuddle, kiss, and I start to drift off with her in my arms. I love her so much, but, as fate would have it, with all the closeness, warmth, kissing, and cuddling, sleep doesn't come immediately. After an hour, we finally lay back, exhausted and spent. More kisses follow, then eventually, we switch off our lights and drift off to the luxurious land of nod—still entwined in each other's arms.

I wake before Scarlett and slowly head to the bathroom, careful not to wake her. She looks so peaceful while she sleeps. I take a hot shower, dress in comfortable clothes pulled from the wardrobe, and think to myself, *when in Rome, do as...*

I pick up the leather-bound binder and quietly head over to the mini-office via the wardrobe, a concept that still feels strange but, clearly, necessary. I settle into the chair and begin going through the documents page by page. I'm eager to find out where Alfred Keynudhia lives. In handwritten black ink, I find a note saying that he resides in a place called Mtwapa—wherever that is—in Mombasa.

I learn that *CODENEINIS INVESTMENTS* is solely run by Alfred Keynudhia and headquartered in Nairobi, Kenya. As I had read last night, the company has a few subsidiaries, including farming and manufacturing, and one of its main earners is coffee exportation. But the real bulk of its income comes from real estate. It owns huge swathes of land, office buildings, residential apartments, houses, and even a few hotels. It's mind-boggling. The company seems to be thriving, and it's hard to wrap my head around the idea that the man behind all this might be my biological father.

I meticulously review each page and come across a declaration from Mr. Keynudhia stating that the company and all its assets will be handed over to his two sons once they each turn 21. I'm not particularly concerned about wealth I never knew existed; what matters to me is that my biological parents might still be alive—and the fact that I have an identical twin brother who apparently knows where I live. According to those two women yesterday, he was seen outside my flat and had even paid them to say nothing. Very odd.

There's more information regarding company branch transfers, and I discover the firm employs over a thousand people. Everything is clearly presented and business-like. I'm no expert in business, but even I can tell Alfred's done very well for himself. What strikes me as strange, though, is that There's no mention of Kathleen—Alex told me she was my biological mother and that she and Alfred had started the company together. But perhaps that detail is buried elsewhere, or maybe it's been omitted for a reason. No matter, I tell myself.

I go over the paperwork again, just to be sure, then zip the binder closed. I unlock the safe and return it. The briefcase is still on the table. I open it, move the money aside, and glance at the neatly folded documents. Aside from that, There's not much else. The paperwork simply confirms that the ensuite is indefinitely booked. I'm not sure what I was expecting to find, but That's that.

I return the briefcase to the safe, lock it, and tiptoe back to the bedroom. Scarlett is still asleep. It's now nine-thirty in the morning, and I feel refreshed after a good night's sleep, ready to face whatever today has in store for yours truly.

I sit at the dining table and decide to do a quick search of Nairobi on my phone. I already know it's Kenya's capital and largest city. I've always been good with world geography, something my university friends often joked about, but I have a thirst for knowledge, especially when it comes to people and places.

I learn that Nairobi is the only city in the world with a national park and that it boasts Africa's fourth-largest stock exchange by trading volume. This catches my attention, possibly because of what I've just learned about CODENEINIS INVESTMENTS. Strange, I've never had much of a head for business.

The internet also tells me that Nairobi is a major cultural and economic hub, and that the Nairobi Securities Exchange is one of the largest and second-oldest on the continent.

Oddly, I find myself drawn to this business side of things, something I wouldn't have even considered a week ago.

Since Alex mentioned my biological parents live along the coast in Mombasa, I search that next. I know it's the second largest city in Kenya after Nairobi, and that it sits along the Indian Ocean. My phone tells me Mombasa was once the capital of British East Africa before Nairobi took over in 1907. *Damn. That's a long time ago*, I think.

It's nicknamed "The White and Blue City," and is the oldest city in the country. Its location on the Indian Ocean made it a key trading hub historically. Today, it's known for tourism and even has its own international airport.

I click away from that and check my emails. I hear rustling in the bed and glance up, Scarlett is sitting up, looking around until she sees me at the dining table.

"Good morning, handsome," she says, yawning and stretching her arms.

Oh, my—she looks so beautiful. I stand up and walk toward her

CHAPTER TWENTY-TWO

On the other side of town, Alex had woken up before six o'clock and had been busy on his computer and phone. He was hoping all his hard work would soon culminate in the successful conclusion of the mission Alfred had entrusted to him. Failure was not an option, not now, not when the goal was in sight. He had done everything asked of him. The only nagging problem was Marcus, who seemed hell-bent on sabotaging Alfred's plans. But Alex wasn't about to let that happen.

He had instructed his team of investigators to be on high alert for Chris, and upon any sighting, to bring him directly to Alex, no exceptions. He needed to ensure Chris's safety. Alfred had done so much for him and his family that Alex couldn't even imagine letting him down. His thoughts wandered briefly to Joe, and how the boy's world had been turned upside down in a matter of hours. But it was for the best. He looked forward to the reunion, Alfred finally meeting his son Joe. And, if Alex had his way, Chris would be part of that moment too.

Alex was well aware that Alfred wasn't a well man. He'd purposely avoided telling Joe that on the first day. It had already been too much information—life-altering, even, and adding that burden would have been cruel. There was something else Alex had withheld from Joe, something that would break his heart when revealed. But it had to be told eventually. Joe couldn't move forward without the full truth.

Alfred had always expressed pride in how Joe's life had turned out. Chris, on the other hand, had taken a different path, one that saddened Alfred deeply. It was painful that the two boys had never met, and Alex was determined to change that. He had the resources and the will.

He'd heard rumours about Chris's state of mind. The man had become elusive, nearly impossible to track, even for Alex's seasoned investigators. Sometimes Chris appeared momentarily; other times he vanished like a phantom, a ghost in the mist. But Alex remained resolute. Nothing would please Alfred more than reuniting with both his sons. Time was running out, and Alex knew it.

He had already broken the initial news to Joe, filled him in on his biological parents, and left the leather-bound binder with the company documents inside the safe, trusting Joe to go through it thoroughly. Joe had always been curious by nature.

Now, Alex continued working diligently at his desk, laser-focused. He'd issued a BOLO, be on the lookout, for Chris, and this time, there was no room for failure. The search had to end.

The phone on his mahogany desk rang. He picked up the handset and listened intently, barely interrupting, taking notes on a blotter pad. The call lasted half an hour, punctuated by short, meaningful responses from Alex. When it ended, he leaned back, let out a breath, and clasped his hands behind his head, cheeks puffed out. It was actually happening. Something that would bring the old man peace, a final joy before the inevitable.

He pushed his swivel chair forward and pressed a button on a touchscreen console to his left. Three screens lit up in front of him. He reviewed them one by one, blotter in hand, clicking through messages on the third screen. He glanced around his well-furnished office, his sanctuary, where plans were formed and operations launched. He owed all of it to Alfred.

Years ago, Alex had been caught in a money laundering scam orchestrated by some Italians posing as tourists. He'd been facing a ten-year sentence. But Alfred had intervened after hearing about his situation. He had visited Alex in remand, and they'd formed a bond, especially after Alfred learned that Alex was born in the same city as his twin sons, and that he was a struggling private investigator. Alfred had attended his court appearance, paid his bond, and somehow—Alex still didn't know how, got all the charges dropped. Alex walked out a free man, reunited with his family, who had been on holiday in Mombasa.

Alfred had invited them to his mansion in Mtwapa. The place was breath-taking. Mtwapa, a beach resort full of luxury hotels, couldn't compare to Alfred's estate near Mtwapa Maweni Beach Pillars. It featured grand architecture, luxurious amenities, and sweeping views of the Indian Ocean. The mansion boasted a private beach, an infinity pool, a gourmet kitchen, and multiple bedrooms with high-end finishes. High ceilings, arched doorways, and detailed craftsmanship spoke to its opulence.

Manicured lawns and elegant landscaping surrounded the home. The private beach had comfortable seating, a grill, and a beach bar. The living rooms had floor-to-ceiling windows framing panoramic ocean views, cosy seating arrangements, and a grand fireplace. A formal dining room featured a large table, fine china, and sparkling chandeliers. The gourmet kitchen had top-tier appliances and an island for entertaining. The bedrooms were luxurious, many with en-suites and private balconies.

The mansion was staffed by a chef, a housekeeper, and two groundskeepers. Security was tight, three gates, two manned by four armed guards, and CCTV cameras everywhere. Two sisters also lived there, though Alex couldn't recall their names. Inside, there was a home theatre, a snooker room, a gym, and a spa.

Alfred had helped stabilize Alex's struggling PI firm, and in return, Alex became his trusted agent, keeping tabs on Joe and now searching for Chris. Alfred had shared the story of his twin sons" birth, how he and Kathleen had fled the country while she was pregnant, how the boys were born in England, kidnapped, and how Alfred had ended up detained in Nairobi.

He had worked in secret to reclaim his businesses, always thinking about his sons. Alfred only hinted at his involvement in real estate and manufacturing. Alex never pried. The man had saved his life.

Now, back in the present, Alex's focus sharpened. Joe had to meet his father. It would be emotional, but it needed to happen. And Chris—he had to be found. The family had to be whole again. Alfred deserved that much.

CHAPTER TWENTY-THREE

I gingerly kiss her and we embrace warmly. She looks into my eyes with those alluring, smouldering eyes and tells me to order breakfast while she gets herself sorted in the bathroom. I look at the menu and size up the array of breakfast options. I don't have to ask her; I know what she likes. She can be a fussy eater at times, but choosing food for her has never been a problem, although I do prefer when she does it herself.

I sit on the bed and peruse the menu. There's a variety: continental options, English breakfast, and more specialised choices like Chinese and Japanese breakfasts. The continental breakfast includes pastries, toast, butter, preserves, fruit salad, and yoghurt. More hearty options follow: eggs, bacon, sausage, baked beans, and hash browns. There are also à la carte items like eggs any style, omelettes, and avocado toast. I place the order for both of us. I love coffee and get some for myself, and tea for her.

After attending to her personal care, Scarlett gets casually dressed in front of me, and she is simply stunning. I am running out of superlatives to describe her. She's slipped on a silk brocade that flatters her Nubian skin and highlights her endless curves. Barefoot, with hair cascading like honey, she has me dreaming. We settle at the dining table and enjoy our breakfast, making small talk as we eat, not really focusing on the day ahead.

Later, once the breakfast is cleared away, I take her into the mini office and fill her in on what I've read. She's astounded at the size and complexity of the company. We go over some of the documents again when my phone rings, it's Alex. He tells me he's on his way to the hotel and has a lot planned for today. He says we'll need our passports.

Scarlett's passport is at her house, so we'll need to stop there. Alex arrives twenty minutes later, accompanied by two men I've never seen before. They carry two suitcases and two carry-on bags, which they place on the floor before quietly exiting. Alex, dressed in a brown suit and carrying a black briefcase, gives Scarlett a courteous kiss on the cheek and takes a seat.

"I realise you must be in shock after reading the material I left you," he begins after we sit down. Scarlett holds my right hand in hers.

"I had a phone call this morning from your father," he says, looking at me. "He wants you to fly out to Mombasa. He's eager to meet you. He knows about Scarlett and would be honoured to meet her."

This sounds interesting. I know Mombasa is a coastal city in Kenya—known for its beaches. Scarlett and I are on annual leave, and what better way to spend it than at a beach resort we don't even have to pay for?

Scarlett squeezes my hand and nods.

"In case you're wondering about Scarlett's parents, I've already spoken with them. They're happy for her to accompany you. Inside this briefcase are your passports and tickets. The documents include the necessary visas, and your flight departs at 8 p.m. tonight," he says, spinning the briefcase around to face me.

Inside are two white manila envelopes.

"In the suitcases," he continues, pointing, "you'll find everything you need, clothing, accessories, essentials. Feel free to add or remove items."

"I have to go home and see my parents first," Scarlett says, squeezing my hand again.

"Of course," Alex replies, stretching. "Let's head over there now."

We busy ourselves getting ready, checking phones and chargers. I glance at the wardrobe where the mini-office is. As if reading my mind, Alex walks over and says, "Don't worry about the stuff in here. You won't need it. I'll handle it. There's money inside the envelopes, and several limitless credit cards from your father. Two thousand pounds in cash for duty-free shopping, too."

An hour later, we're at Scarlett's house. I've always liked coming here. Her home is humble and minimalistic, just my style. The living room is functional and airy, full of natural light, enhanced by integrated lighting and sound systems. There's art, textures, and subtle décor. Built-in cabinetry hides clutter. It's warm and welcoming.

Her parents sit on a plush black leather sofa while Alex outlines the plan—Scarlett and I are going to Mombasa to visit a relative for at least two weeks. Her parents, Paulina and Richard, are religious and very proud of Scarlett. They emigrated from Kenya to England in the 1970s, after Kenya gained independence. They've lived a simple, successful life and raised Scarlett with love.

Paulina works at the hospital and Richard now runs a taxi company after retiring from commodities trading. They waited to start a family until they were financially secure, which explains Scarlett being an only child. She often says she wishes she had siblings.

Scarlett and I sit opposite them, not holding hands out of respect. After Alex finishes explaining, he says the driver will remain outside to take us to the airport, then he has to leave.

He pulls me aside, putting an arm around my shoulder.

"Everything will be okay, Joe," he says. "Your father will be waiting. He's seen pictures of you and Scarlett. You're in safe hands."

We shake hands, and he departs.

An hour later, we're around Scarlett's dining table, enjoying lamb chops grilled by her dad, with green vegetables, ugali, and a side of kachumbari. After clearing the table, something I always insist on helping with, we relocate to the study.

Scarlett sips tea while I nurse a glass of orange juice. We examine the plane tickets: London Heathrow to Moi International Airport in Mombasa, via Nairobi. A nine-hour flight, a short layover, and then a quick hop to the coast.

We've checked the suitcases Alex sent. They're packed with everything—beachwear, formal attire, personal items. Sunscreen, insect repellent, hats, sunglasses. The carry-on bags have lotions, socks, books. I pack *A Thousand Splendid Suns* by Khaled Hosseini.

We're driven to Heathrow in Alex's car. The trip takes about two hours through the city's infamously mad traffic. The journey has begun.

CHAPTER TWENTY-FOUR

The airport is situated in Hounslow, fourteen miles west of central London. It is the busiest and largest airport in the UK, as well as one of the busiest in the world. The driver follows traffic snaking through the busy terminal roads and has said only a few words since we left Scarlett's house.

After we are dropped off at Terminal Four, we grab a trolley and load our suitcases and carry-on cases, then head for departures. Since Alex already checked us in online, we proceed through security with our boarding passes and passports.

We're stopped just after security by a stewardess with one of the widest smiles I've ever seen. She inspects our tickets and beckons us to follow her. We fall into line, tugging our carry-ons behind us, and I begin to wonder what the next surprise will be. I'm quickly running out of ways to describe how wildly events have unfolded lately.

We arrive at the Plaza Business Class lounge, where the stewardess ushers us into plush seats and brings us champagne, and we couldn't be happier. I'd almost forgotten we were flying first class. It's clearly obvious Scarlett and I have never flown before.

We're offered a choice of beef, chicken, or vegetarian meals, but we politely decline since we ate enough at Scarlett's house. When it's time to board the Boeing 737–800, we're among the first to step onto the aircraft and are directed to our first-class seats, designed with ergonomic precision to enhance comfort. Scarlett and I settle in. My thoughts spiral.

I imagine all sorts of scenarios: what will happen when we land in Mombasa, what I'll say to the man who is apparently my biological father and the woman who may be my biological mother. Even though I don't know who Chris is, I silently wish he were here with me, on this strange journey of discovery.

After everyone boards and the cabin begins to quieten, the pilot's voice echoes around us from unseen speakers. His voice is booming yet smooth, as he welcomes us on board. He reminds everyone to fasten seatbelts, secure any carry-on baggage, and ensure that tray tables are in the upright position for take-off. He points out the safety information card in the seat pockets and highlights emergency exits.

He announces our destination, Jomo Kenyatta International Airport in Nairobi, and mentions that the flight will take around nine hours and ten minutes. The weather in Nairobi is reportedly favourable, with a temperature of thirty degrees Celsius. He cautions there might be light turbulence and asks passengers to follow the crew's instructions when necessary. He concludes by inviting everyone to sit back, relax, and enjoy the flight.

The aircraft taxis toward the runway and aligns along the centreline. The pilot advances the throttles and we begin our take-off roll. The acceleration is intense but muted by the plush surroundings of our first-class seats. As the aircraft reaches rotation speed, the pilot lifts the nose, and the jet leaves the tarmac, climbing smoothly toward cruising altitude.

"What's wrong, honey?" Scarlett asks gently, reaching for my hand. She knows me too well. She can always tell when something's on my mind, and I love her all the more for it.

I look at her beautiful face, already creased with concern. "It's the not knowing and the knowing," I say, softly brushing her cheek. "I'm going to meet my real parents, and I have no idea what I'm going to say, or do, when I meet them."

She squeezes my hand without speaking at first, then locks eyes with me. "Darling, the right words will come at the right time. Don't worry yourself sick. Just take it step by step. And remember, I'm right here with you."

She leans in and kisses me, cupping my face in her hands. If only life had stayed this simple, I think, as I return her kiss.

Later, we're offered soft drinks and, after chatting for a couple of hours, we decide to get some sleep in preparation for What's ahead. First-class (or business class, as the airline labels it) provides flat-bed seating—and I can confirm it's incredibly comfortable. Scarlett appears to be enjoying hers.

The flight is smooth. There's little turbulence, and Scarlett sleeps through most of it. I, on the other hand, find sleep difficult. Thoughts race through my mind as we edge closer to our destination. The cabin crew are friendly, attentive, and offer food and drinks throughout the flight.

In my head, I drift to work, strangely enough. I find myself missing my patients and my colleagues. I love my job. I love seeing patients who arrive in psychological crisis begin the journey toward recovery. I've formed real connections with some of them, and There's no better feeling than seeing someone discharged in far better condition than when they arrived.

Maybe I'm thinking about work because, up here at 36,000 feet, I feel helpless. When I'm at work, I have control. But right now? I'm being moved by forces beyond my control. Like a puppet, and Alex is holding the strings.

Still, Alex hasn't given me reason to distrust him. He arranged the suite at the Hilton. He gave me money he didn't have to. He's been upfront. Maybe…just maybe…he's on the level.

Let's wait and see, a quiet voice inside me says.

I must've drifted off because I wake to someone shaking my shoulder. It's Scarlett, smiling under her blanket, her knees pulled up on the flat-bed.

She's laughing, and I'm still groggy.

"What's so funny?" I mumble, rubbing my eyes.

"You did it again," she says.

I blink, confused.

"You were talking in your sleep. Loudly. I had to wake you to check if you were okay."

It's not unusual, I've done that before, but it hasn't happened for a while, according to Scarlett.

"I know you're worried," she says gently. "But don't stress. It's going to be alright."

A steward arrives, offering breakfast. We choose a continental meal with freshly prepared snacks, tea, and coffee. Soon after, the captain announces we'll be landing shortly. He gives us the local time, the weather, and asks everyone to fasten seatbelts.

We have a two-and-a-half-hour layover in Nairobi. We don't leave the airport—it's a short stop, so we browse the duty-free shops near our gate. We admire the local curios, hand-carved wooden figurines of Maasai warriors, and vivid paintings of tribal life. Scarlett is fascinated by the multi-coloured beadwork, especially the vibrant combinations used in traditional Kenyan jewellery.

I browse through the greeting cards and decide to buy two, for my parents in England. It still feels strange saying that now. But they are my real parents, the ones who raised me, loved me, gave me the best start in life.

This is going to be complicated, I can already tell. My heart tells me that emotions will be running high on both sides. I can't even begin to imagine what my biological parents must be feeling, knowing that at least one of their sons is on the way to meet them today.

I pay for the two cards and the selection of beads Scarlett has picked out. The colours, green, white, black, and red, match the Kenyan national flag. I'm proud of her choice.

Then I spot wristbands in the same colours and buy six—two for Scarlett and me, two for my parents, and two for hers. We grab some drinks and head to the gate for our final flight, to Mombasa.

The second plane is smaller, and the flight lasts just over an hour. As we begin our descent into Moi International Airport, I've mustered the courage I need. Whatever's ahead, I'm ready.

I squeeze Scarlett's hand tightly. As the plane taxis along the runway, I exhale deeply. We're almost there. Passengers begin disembarking. I suggest Scarlett and I hang back, we're in no rush.

Once the plane empties, we grab our carry-on bags and make our way to the exit. The cabin crew wish us a pleasant stay as we step off the aircraft and onto the gangway.

And then, a voice.

"Welcome to Kenya, Joe and Scarlett."

I turn. Standing near a group of officials by the gangway, grinning broadly with arms outstretched, is Alex, The private investigator.

CHAPTER TWENTY-FIVE

The street looked deserted at this time of evening. It was dark, and the street lights couldn't properly illuminate every part. There was little traffic, and most cars sped away slightly over the speed limit. Only a few windows were lit from inside. Most shops were dimly lit with two exceptions: one was a mini-market convenience store, and the other was a closed shop whose lights remained on, prompting one to wonder whether someone had forgotten to switch them off or if someone was inside doing goodness knows what. If one waited long enough, a couple of rats could be seen scurrying along the kerbside, rummaging for food.

A hooded figure in the shadows took a long drag from a cigarette that hung from the side of his mouth, his right hand deep in the pocket of his tracksuit bottoms. He leaned against a railing by the side of the road, staying within the shadows, either avoiding someone or waiting for something. His mind was a whirlwind of thoughts as he contemplated his next move, hoping it would bring all the madness to an end. He took another drag, dropped the cigarette to the pavement, stepped forward, and crushed it underfoot with his black trainers. He appeared like a silhouette, an outline darker than the dim background, partially hidden by the enveloping shadows. His hood obscured his face, giving him an air of anonymity. The black hoodie and matching tracksuit bottoms only added to the sense of concealment, rendering him unrecognizable. He could have easily been mistaken for someone trying to stay warm or simply avoiding recognition.

But that wasn't the case. Chris adjusted the black rucksack on his back, glanced at the watch on his right wrist (he always wore it on the right), and scanned the darkening street. A faint hum buzzed from the back pocket of his rucksack, it was his Samsung mobile phone alerting him that the battery was down to ten percent. He had a good relationship with his phone, which had never let him down. He made a mental note to "feed it" by charging it as soon as possible.

He appeared composed, like a man on a mission, his own mission. As he mentally counted down, he anticipated the arrival of the person he was waiting for, and his apprehension mounted. At twenty-one, Chris had experienced more than most people twice his age. He'd had a rough start in life, bouncing from one foster home to another.

His thoughts were interrupted by the sound of approaching footsteps. He turned toward the noise and saw what he had been expecting: Jorum, all seven feet of him, striding confidently toward him like Goliath heading into battle. He exuded the kind of composure that came with being unshakable.

Without a word, Jorum fished through a large grey holdall and pulled out a brown manila envelope, which he handed to Chris. Chris took the envelope and tucked it into his black rucksack, which he had swung around from his back. He gave Jorum an appraising look.

Before Chris could speak, Jorum warned, "You better be really careful. He has guard dogs now and won't hesitate to let them loose. He's getting more paranoid every day, obsessed with getting you back. Something about everything coming to a close soon. And just as well that—"

Chris cut him off with a raised hand, signalling silence. He liked Jorum, all 250 pounds of muscle, not an ounce of fat on him. The man hit the gym five times a week, ran ten miles every evening, and could eat enough for three in one sitting. But while Jorum had been blessed physically, he lacked mental sharpness. He followed orders to the letter, incapable of thinking for himself—which suited Chris perfectly. He could manipulate Jorum to get whatever he needed.

Jorum wore an all-yellow tracksuit and matching trainers, his usual running gear. Chris silently questioned his choice of colour, but then again, that was just Jorum. A giant in every sense, Jorum had close-cropped black hair, dark brown eyes, and a face as sinister as the devil himself, a comparison other often made in jest, and which Jorum surprisingly found amusing. He had a good personality, but Chris could never stand the way he spoke, like a horse race commentator.

"Thanks, brother. I won't forget this," Chris said, extending a hand. Jorum shook it firmly, nearly crushing Chris's fingers, then grinned and disappeared into the darkness.

Chris tightened his rucksack straps and walked in the opposite direction. He knew he couldn't let anyone know where he lived; Marcus was relentless in his pursuit, blaming him for a botched drug deal Chris had nothing to do with. Chris detested drugs, anything that altered his thinking.

He constantly checked behind him as he walked. After twenty minutes, he reached what looked like an abandoned warehouse. Its decaying brick walls were cracked, its boarded-up windows vandalized and filthy. Satisfied he was alone, Chris pushed aside a wooden partition, once a fence, to create an entry point, slipped inside, and pulled the partition back into place.

Inside, he pulled out a high-powered torch from his rucksack, illuminating the space before him. The air was thick with a musty smell. Floorboards creaked and groaned beneath his steps. He passed through a maze of disused rooms, strewn with old machinery and graffiti. The brick walls crumbled in places, with missing bricks and peeling mortar. Spider web cracks ran across the surface. Some windows had bars, others were shattered or missing, letting in cold drafts. Moss and weeds grew on exposed roof timbers, and the air reeked of damp decay.

Yet Chris wasn't fazed. He'd lived through worse. This place, as derelict as it was, served a purpose, it was somewhere Marcus would never think to look. The warehouse leaned in on itself, and Chris often referred to its crooked walls as his "leaning walls of Chrisdom."

He reached his destination: a large room at the far end with an intact steel door. From his rucksack, he retrieved a long metal key. Covering his mouth from the mildew stench, he unlocked the door, stepped inside, and locked it behind him.

The interior bore no resemblance to the world he'd just exited. At first glance, it looked like a mini-communications centre, with an array of equipment neatly organized. Chris placed his rucksack and key on a sleek maple desk and moved to a white door, which opened to reveal a simple bedroom. He removed his shoes, set them on a beige rug, and returned to the desk area.

The room was arranged for maximum efficiency. Cables were tucked neatly to avoid clutter, and basic air conditioning maintained stable temperatures. The hidden power supply was expertly rigged; no one would guess it existed in a derelict warehouse.

Three computer screens lined the desk. Below them sat a PlayStation 5 and a police scanner. A black swivel chair rested nearby. There wasn't much furniture, but the room had essentials: a mini fridge-freezer, cooking hob, kettle, microwave, and a three-tier trolley that held sugar, coffee, a cup, a plate, a spoon, and two massive mineral water containers.

A single light bulb hung from the low ceiling, casting a steady glow. Chris sat at the desk, plugged in his Samsung phone to charge beside the third monitor, and powered up the middle screen. All three sprang to life with glowing green numerals like something out of The Matrix. While the system booted, he flicked on the kettle and stepped back into the small bedroom.

Instead of a bed, a canvas hammock stretched across the room. Most would see it as a place for naps, but for Chris, it was for planning. A nearby inflatable air mattress, his "blow-up bed", was a portable setup made from urethane plastic. He liked the idea of "blowing up" Marcus.

Two silver suitcases, one large and one small, sat next to the mattress. Nearby were blue sandals and two pairs of shoes, one black, the other dark tan. Chris removed his hoodie, revealing a black T-shirt, slipped into his sandals, and returned to the main room to prepare his coffee.

He stirred in a teaspoon of sugar and surveyed the space, his eyes landing on three large plastic containers in a corner. He knew they would come in handy. Reflecting on his life, Chris wondered how he had made it this far.

He'd spent his early years bounced from one foster home to another. One of the worst times had been when he was sent to the North West, a place he despised. Settling in at the desk with his hot coffee, he hit a key on his keyboard and leaned back, waiting for his program to load.

Chris had always wondered why his childhood had been so harsh. He'd rebelled against most foster parents, being the only Black child in white families had led to bullying, especially in school. He couldn't understand why he hadn't been placed with a family of his own ethnicity. He'd frequently run away, sometimes ending up sleeping rough. He got in trouble for shoplifting. At ten, he started smoking marijuana. By fifteen, he was part of a gang involved in burglary and vandalism. He had been in and out of Young Offender Institutions.

Despite everything, he still knew very little about his biological parents. It was clear he wasn't white, yet whenever he asked about his origins, he was met with silence.

CHAPTER TWENTY-SIX

He had then been persuaded to start selling marijuana to school children, which had again landed him in the Young Offenders Institute. After he was released, he vowed never to set foot in such a place again. As fate would have it, he met Marcus, who was known as an "uncle" to some of his friends. Chris had been invited to Marcus's house in the South East part of London on weekends, and he really liked the place, huge, gated, spacious, with plenty of food and drink. He could stay over any time he wanted. Marcus encouraged the teenagers to call him "uncle" and appeared to cater to their every need.

Unbeknownst to Chris, most of Marcus's "nephews" were selling hard drugs for him. Chris learned this when he turned sixteen. One day, Marcus summoned him to his study in the mansion and said that since he'd been so generous to Chris, he expected something in return. Chris was at a loss. What could he possibly offer to a man who seemed to have everything, five-bedroom house, three cars, endless money, bodyguards, and a life of luxury?

Chris sat there in silence and apprehension, not comprehending what Marcus wanted. Marcus then began making sexual advances, which Chris vehemently rejected. But as days wore on, Chris realised he couldn't even leave the house, Marcus's bodyguards prevented it. One night, Marcus spiked his drink. Chris passed out and woke up naked in Marcus's bed, with Marcus asleep beside him. He fled the room, but that nightmare became a routine for a year. Marcus threatened to make him disappear if he refused him.

This devastated Chris's mental health. He was hospitalised several times, but Marcus always stayed close, ensuring Chris never revealed the abuse to mental health professionals. By seventeen, Marcus had sent him to sell hard drugs—but never alone. Chris was always watched. Marcus claimed Chris was his "special nephew" and had bigger plans for him.

Chris couldn't figure Marcus out. As a Black man, he should have been a father figure, but he behaved worse than the worst foster families. Chris vowed he'd one day take revenge; Marcus would never see it coming. He kept tabs on Marcus's bodyguards and noticed one, Jorum, a hulking but polite man, treated him with respect. Chris hated how Marcus mocked Jorum, calling him "Tweedledumb who had swallowed Tweedledumber." Chris hoped to be sent out with Jorum, knowing he could easily slip away.

One day, Marcus left his study door ajar. Chris, under orders to wait outside for daily instructions, sat there while Marcus nursed a hangover from the night before. Alphonso, the chief bodyguard, had locked all the doors for Marcus's "safety." That morning, Marcus met with two men. Chris recognised one, Sam, who had always been kind to him. Sam once winked while saying he was just an "acquaintance" of Marcus, a gesture Chris hadn't understood then.

That morning, Marcus must have forgotten his rules because Chris overheard everything. What he heard shocked him to his core. Marcus spoke about Chris having a twin brother named Joe, living in the city. Their biological father, referred to as Alf, was a very wealthy man living in Mombasa, Kenya. The twins were heirs to a vast empire, and rumours suggested Alf was not long for this world.

Chris memorised the names and Joe's address. He also learned that Marcus planned to seize the father's business empire. The biological father, Alfred Keynudhia, had been betrayed by Marcus to their home country's government. He was falsely accused of plotting a coup, forcing him and his pregnant wife Cathy to flee to England—where Joe and Chris were born.

But Marcus hadn't stopped. He collaborated with corrupt officials, seized Alfred's businesses, and located the family in England. One night, Alfred and his wife were abducted and flown back. The twins were adopted by separate families. Chris heard Joe was raised by a good, God-fearing family, attended good schools, and had a happy childhood.

Chris couldn't believe all he was hearing. He stayed rooted to the spot, absorbing every word. When the meeting ended, he quietly slipped back to his room. From that day on, Chris struggled to even look at Marcus, who continued using him for drug deals, always with an armed escort. Chris began plotting his escape, even if it meant eliminating his handler.

Back in the present, Chris looked at the programme on the screen, satisfied that Marcus's men would never find him in this secure location. He clicked on a link about CODENEINIS INVESTMENTS, owned by Alfred Keynudhia. The company was massive. If all this were true, his life could change forever.

Photos of Alfred with ministers, investors, and at press conferences filled the screen. Chris saw similarities in their features and was staggered. The only mention of family was of a wife, Kathleen Keynudhia, said to have helped found the company. There were no pictures of her, and Chris felt a pang of sadness, he wouldn't be able to see a photo of the woman who might be his biological mother.

He placed his cup of coffee on the desk and typed on his keyboard. Logging into his bank account, he checked the deposited funds. He had to stretch every penny if his plan was to succeed. He walked to the maple desk, reached into his black rucksack, and pulled out two manila envelopes. Sitting back at his desk, he opened one envelope, removing a passport and airline tickets. He placed both on the desk.

The tickets were for a flight from London Gatwick to Addis Ababa, Ethiopia, nonstop, seven hours and forty minutes on Ethiopian Airlines. Chris placed the tickets inside the passport, which bore his full name and date of birth. He had learned to drive during his rough teenage years when he and his gang stole cars for joyrides, though Marcus had never allowed him to get a license. But Chris had demanded a birth certificate from one foster home, threatening consequences. With it, he got a passport at sixteen and opened a Barclays account to prepare for escape.

Despite everything, Chris loved books. Marcus had a small library, more for show than use. Chris spent hours there when Marcus didn't need him. Marcus, thinking Chris was keeping to himself, was pleased, unaware that Chris was soaking up knowledge like a sponge, especially in electrical engineering.

He read texts, researched online, and discovered that electrical engineers design, develop, and maintain systems in various sectors, energy, transport, construction. Problem-solving, technical skill, and precision were key. Back in the present, Chris admired the rigging he had installed to power and ventilate his underground bunker. It had taken time, but he'd built it all himself.

He shook off the memories. Marcus no longer owned him. He was on a mission. Forgiveness was impossible for someone like Marcus.

Things are different now, Chris thought. He set aside the passport and tickets, pulled a wad of £20 notes from the other envelope, counted them, and smiled. A set of keys fell out, which he pocketed. His phone beeped, it was fully charged. He unplugged it, leaned back in his chair, and scrolled through the calendar.

"It is time," he said to himself, eyes locked on the chosen date.

CHAPTER TWENTY-SEVEN

I look at Alex in disbelief as he gently hugs Scarlett and me, still smiling his wide smile. Before I can ask any questions, Alex ushers us away from the plane's entrance, and we start walking along the gangway toward what I'm sure is the arrivals terminal.

Alex is wearing comfortable khaki beach shorts, a loose white T-shirt, dark sunglasses, a white baseball cap, and brown sandals. Who in their right mind goes to an airport dressed like that? He really has to stop appearing out of nowhere unannounced.

"I bet you're wondering how I got here before you," he says, helping Scarlett with her carry-on case.

"Well," I reply, "is there any point in asking, since you're already here?" I walk alongside him, Scarlett on my right, Alex just ahead on my left, leading the way.

"After I checked you guys in online, I headed over to Heathrow and hopped on a British Airways flight. Got to Nairobi and arrived here just over four hours ago," he explains as we continue walking.

The heat inside the terminal is noticeable, just as the travel leaflets described. Terminal 1, primarily for international flights, features two levels, around twenty-four check-in counters, and ample seating, food, and retail options. I never quite understand how I get so particular about small details in life. Scarlett says I'm pedantic.

Alex stops and asks for our passports as we near immigration. He heads to a side office, leaving Scarlett and me to settle on some comfortable seats. Travelers are lining up at the immigration desk, eager to begin whatever brought them to Mombasa.

While he's gone, Scarlett pulls out her phone and remarks that the signal is surprisingly good. We'd enabled data roaming during our Nairobi stopover so we could connect to local networks and use our phones freely. Scarlett's texting her mum now, and I take that as a cue to message mine.

I still acknowledge them as my parents—the only ones I've known. They raised me and gave me the best start in life. I send a quick message. Nothing elaborate. Texts are for getting things done. Three minutes later, my mum replies, wishing me all the best and reminding me they love me no matter what. I couldn't agree more. I pocket my phone and lean back, taking in my surroundings.

I've always had a thing for situational awareness. There's a large sign making it clear that the Kenya Airports Authority (KAA) manages the airport's infrastructure, safety, and security. I like knowing about places I go to, collecting as much information as I can. Scarlett often jokes I have the mind of an elephant—and a photographic memory. I don't know how I retain so much, even from brief visits. Apparently, at this airport, ground handling is managed by private franchises, so their uniforms depend on the company, while KAA staff follow standard dress codes.

Just then, Alex reappears with a man in a dark grey suit, white shirt, and black tie. They're laughing, clearly familiar with each other. The man slaps Alex on the back playfully.

Alex holds our documents in his right hand as they walk over.

The man introduces himself as Geoffrey and shakes our hands warmly, welcoming us to Mombasa. He's light-skinned, about five foot six, around 175 pounds, and wearing dark sunglasses. He gestures for us to follow him. We veer off from the immigration queue. Alex, still chatting with Geoffrey, takes Scarlett's carry-on again, and we move deeper into the airport. I hold Scarlett's hand.

Soon we find ourselves in a hangar. Through the wide open doors, I see a helicopter with its blades slowly rotating and the door open. The outside heat hits like a furnace, like we just walked into an oven. A digital display near the exit reads thirty degrees Celsius. Damn. I've never felt such heat. Scarlett and I huddle together, both visibly uncomfortable.

"This is the helicopter that will take you to Mtwapa," Geoffrey announces as a man in a flight suit approaches. Geoffrey introduces him as Ivan, our pilot.

Ivan. Russian? In Africa? He's wearing a Nomex flight suit and looks middle-aged, with blond hair and very fair skin. About six feet tall, clearly athletic, he shakes our hands and greets us in a surprisingly American-sounding accent.

Scarlett and I exchange looks. This trip is growing more adventurous by the minute. If this were a proper holiday, I'd be snapping pictures like mad, but it doesn't feel like a holiday. A helicopter. Great. I've always had a fear of heights, something Scarlett teases me about every time we get in an elevator. Flying in a helicopter? Not ideal.

Ivan leads us to the aircraft, and as we exit the hangar, another man, short, Black, with cropped hair, takes our carry-on cases and walks them to the helicopter.

We follow, and soon Scarlett, Alex, and I are strapped in. We're handed flight helmets, "skull domes," apparently, for the duration of the trip. At least inside, we've escaped the searing heat. I can't believe people work outside in that weather. I see men in high-vis jackets on the tarmac moving about their duties.

To distract myself, I grab an information folder from beside my seat. Scarlett, aware of my height phobia, holds my hand tightly.

"I'm here, sweetie," she whispers.

I nod and focus on the folder. It says the blades rotate due to a combination of flapping and feathering, key for lift control and balance. It also mentions lead-lag movements for stability. I don't care what any of it means, I just need something to focus on besides the altitude.

Ivan announces that the trip to Mtwapa is 24.5 kilometres and should only take a few minutes. I do a quick mental conversion, about 15 miles. Not far.

Alex looks completely at ease in his beach attire, like he just came from sipping cocktails. The folder also identifies our helicopter as an Airbus EC120 Colibri, five seats, single engine, single main rotor.

We lift off. Ivan points out landmarks, but the journey is short. We leave Mombasa County and enter Kilifi County. I refuse to look outside. Scarlett and Alex are pointing things out, the Indian Ocean, among them.

"We're coming in to land," Ivan says. My anxiety spikes. This is it.

Alex looks excited. I wish I shared that feeling. Scarlett leans in, her helmet pressing against mine.

"We're almost there, sweetie. The next chapter of your life. I'm right here by your side, darling," she whispers, squeezing my hand.

I slide the information folder back into its slot and glance at Alex. He's been watching me the entire time. He leans forward, squeezes my shoulder, and says, "We're here, Joe. This is where it ends, my friend."

He couldn't be more wrong.

I brace myself. After everything, from England to Nairobi and now Mombasa, it's time to face the truth.

One part of me wishes I had never met Alex. The other says it's all been worth it.

If I'm truly going to meet my biological parents... this isn't the end.

This is where it all begins.

CHAPTER TWENTY-EIGHT

Chris stood up and walked over to his small bedroom, opening the larger of the two silver suitcases. It was packed with a variety of clothes suited for warm climates. He did a quick inspection of its contents, then zipped it up and moved on to the smaller suitcase.

This one contained paperwork. He sat on his air mattress, pulled out a few documents, and began reading. After about twenty-five minutes, he rummaged through the papers again, selected a few, and glanced at his watch. It was almost 11 p.m. Chris walked over to the area with the computer screens, reached for his black rucksack, opened it, and stuffed the papers from the suitcase inside. From a back pocket, he took out a tube of toothpaste and a plastic cup, brushed his teeth, rinsed with mineral water, and poured the waste into a small bucket in the corner. He shut down the computer and returned to his sleeping area, soon falling asleep with his mobile phone by his side.

Chris woke up around six in the morning. He knew today was important and wanted to feel refreshed before getting to work. After getting dressed in black jeans, black trainers, and a blue top, he moved the silver suitcases into the main room and deflated the air mattress. He dismantled the hammock, gathered any remaining items, and placed them all neatly into the three storage containers. He disposed of the mini fridge, cooking hob, kettle, microwave, and anything else that might reveal someone had been staying there. These items were scattered in hard-to-reach parts of the disused warehouse where discovery was unlikely.

Locking the metal door behind him, Chris grabbed his black rucksack and left the warehouse with one goal in mind: to steal a van and move his belongings to a storage facility. He had already leased space for three months. Chris had learned how to start cars during his time with a gang years ago. He knew of a garage tucked away on Cloverdale Street that didn't open until 11 a.m. It sat at the end of a cul-de-sac in a nondescript area. From previous scouting, he knew the place was quiet on Saturday mornings.

He found the white van, walked past it casually, and tested the driver's door. It was unlocked, just as it had been a week earlier when he first spotted it. He slipped inside, pulled a screwdriver from his back pocket, and inserted it into the keyhole. Then, using a small metal rod from his front pocket, he gently tapped the screwdriver to break the ignition pins, turned it, and started the diesel engine. He noticed the fuel gauge wasn't working, but he wasn't too concerned.

Suddenly, a face appeared at the passenger window. An older white man was trying to open the door, shouting, "Let me in! You have to let me in!"

Startled, Chris put the van in first gear and drove off, sending the man sprawling as he disappeared down the street.

By 4 p.m., Chris was at Victoria Station. He had successfully stored his belongings in a massive Limelight warehouse operated by Big Y Storage and was satisfied everything was going as planned. He had briefly considered heading to South East London, but whatever he had in mind now felt more important.

He looked at the departure display. The train to Gatwick was leaving in fifteen minutes. Chris made his way to the platform. The Gatwick Express, a direct train between London Victoria, Gatwick Airport, Haywards Heath, and Brighton, wasn't something Chris cared much about beyond its function.

The journey to Gatwick took roughly thirty minutes. Chris leaned back in his seat, eyes closed, his large silver suitcase beside him and his black rucksack on his lap.

Gatwick Airport is located south of London in Crawley, West Sussex, around twenty-eight miles from the city centre. It's connected via the M23 motorway and has a direct rail link to Victoria. Chris double-checked his ticket, he had three and a half hours until departure. He began navigating toward the North Terminal.

Flying economy, this would be Chris's first time flying, and leaving the country. He hoped all his plans would pay off. The terminal had various shops, restaurants, and services. As he pushed his trolley with the silver suitcase, he noticed premium lounges like No1 Lounge and Club Aspire offering complimentary food and drinks. He wasn't hungry, he'd always found it curious that he could go all day on one meal without needing more.

He wanted to check in early to avoid rushing. He knew the airline's counters closed one hour before departure.

Chris was dozing in the departure lounge when a female voice over the tannoy announced that the Ethiopian Airlines flight was ready to board. He rubbed his eyes, stretched, and joined the crowd heading to gate 568.

Once passengers boarded and began settling in, the pilot made his welcome announcement. The flight was bound for Addis Ababa, estimated at seven hours and forty-five minutes. Weather conditions in Addis were described as welcoming, with temperatures around 31°C. The pilot also warned of potential turbulence and asked passengers to follow crew instructions.

Chris couldn't help but notice the beauty of the female crew members. When they delivered safety instructions, including information on seatbelts, electronic devices, carry-on baggage, and emergency procedures, he paid attention, mostly because they were delivered by two stunning Ethiopian women.

Shortly after take-off, the cabin filled with quiet conversation in multiple languages. Mothers secured their children, and a few passengers offered prayers aloud. The crew moved efficiently through the cabin, offering food options. Chris noticed they catered to different tastes and dietary needs. He saw a menu offering both international dishes and Ethiopian cuisine. Economy passengers were served hot meals and snacks, including a version of the national dish, a flavourful stew with Injera, a traditional flatbread. Chris wasn't hungry and wrapped himself in the provided blanket, drifting off to sleep.

CHAPTER TWENTY-NINE

Ivan gently glides the Airbus EC120 Colibri down onto a helipad nestled within what can only be described as a fairy-tale mansion on a sprawling estate. From inside the helicopter, I stare at the most beautiful house I've ever laid eyes on, if buildings can indeed be called beautiful. I'm at a loss for words as the helicopter hovers briefly before Ivan brings it to a smooth, controlled landing. Strangely, my fear of heights is no longer in focus. We're on solid ground, and I'm fully aware that whatever lies ahead may determine the rest of my life.

This is a leap of faith, led by Alex, the ever-composed private investigator, and I'm grateful he's here. Even more reassuring is the presence of Scarlett, the love of my life, seated beside me. We remove our flight helmets and, holding each other tightly, share a quiet, intimate moment, our foreheads almost touching.

She squeezes my left hand and whispers, "It's time you found out, my darling." A smile spreads across her face, and somehow, I feel at ease.

Ivan, now outside, opens the helicopter door. Alex disembarks first, his demeanour sober but still wearing that familiar wide grin. Scarlett and I step out, hand in hand, and are immediately struck by the relentless heat. Two casually dressed men, wearing loose t-shirts, trousers, and sandals, approach the helicopter and collect our luggage. They begin walking toward the mansion along a tarmac path flanked by small lamps and a perfectly manicured lawn.

The estate is immaculate.

As we move forward, two young women approach. They're dressed in long, flowing gowns that trail behind them, wearing white sandals and carrying fresh bouquets. They bow slightly.

"Welcome to Mtwapa," one says, offering the flowers to Scarlett and me.

We accept them, and I glance at Alex. "These ladies will take us inside," he says, flashing a wide smile. Scarlett and I follow, clutching the fragrant flowers as Alex walks alongside, striking up a polite conversation. Ivan remains with his helicopter on the helipad, and around us is nothing but tranquil beauty.

The mansion is embraced by its surroundings, as if nature itself had designed the estate around it. At the entrance, the two women step aside. Alex gestures for me to enter first. I cross the threshold, Scarlett close behind.

Inside, an elderly man stands waiting. He wears a white suit over a red polo shirt and silver sandals. His thinning grey hair is neatly combed, his skin smooth and glowing. His brown eyes and small ears, just like mine, catch me off guard. I'm looking at an older version of myself.

He walks toward me, arms open wide, and embraces me in a powerful, affectionate hug.

"Welcome to Kenya, my son," he says.

I catch the scent of expensive aftershave and feel the strength in his arms. I hug him back, unsure what to say.

After a moment, he steps back and studies me from head to toe, joy brimming in his eyes.

Turning to Scarlett, he offers a gentlemanly bow and kisses her hand. "And you must be the lovely Scarlett."

She smiles, responding warmly, "Yes, I am."

He introduces the two women as Allegra and Aurelia, and politely asks them to place the flowers in the sitting room. Once they leave, he takes my hands again and continues looking at me with unmistakable paternal affection. Alex stands quietly beside us, letting the moment unfold.

I manage to say the only thing that comes to mind. "This is a lovely house."

He smiles sincerely. "Let us retire to the main lounge. You must be tired from the journey."

Hand in hand, we walk through what I can only describe as a palace. The high-ceilinged hallway is lined with expensive artwork, leading us to an opulent lounge, a space that blends a living room and family room with plush, sunken sofas. A massive oval glass table dominates the centre, surrounded by silver stools and topped with bronze doilies. Crystal chandeliers hang above us like frozen fireworks.

Scarlett sits beside me. Alex, now barefoot, lounges comfortably on another sofa, clearly familiar with the space. I'm not even sure when he took his sandals off. Funny how the smallest details stand out.

Allegra and Aurelia return with a trolley loaded with drinks, liquor and soft options alike. They place crystal-clear glasses on the golden stools in front of us. The glass rims shimmer like starlight.

Alex grins, spotting a bottle of Macallan 1926 Fine & Rare, the most expensive whisky in the world. He also notes the Yamazaki 55-year-old Japanese whisky and helps himself to the Macallan, calling it his favourite. Scarlett and I are poured pineapple and orange juice, respectively. Alfred, the man who is, undeniably, my father, opts for sparkling mineral water with ice.

"I'd like to welcome you all to my home in Mtwapa," Alfred begins. "The Lord has finally brought one of my sons to me. A prayer I've held in my heart for twenty-one years has been answered."

His voice is deep, calm, and authoritative, measured and resonant, the kind of voice that commands attention naturally.

"My name is Alfred Keynudhia," he says, looking directly into my eyes. "I'm sure Alex has filled you in on much of what brought you here."

I nod, holding Scarlett's hand. She squeezes mine again.

"Age only brings wisdom if the heart remains vulnerable and pure in the most challenging of times," he says, his tone rich with gravitas. "To reach your destination, you must walk, run, drive, fly, sail, do whatever it takes. I've paid my fare in tears, and perhaps That's why some people listen."

I feel a swelling of pride looking at him. He speaks like someone used to addressing large crowds.

"My lovely wife Kathleen isn't with us today," he continues. "I asked Alex not to tell you Kathleen is very ill. She's bedridden. Stage 4 breast cancer. She's been given six months to live."

A heaviness descends on the room.

Alfred's face remains unreadable, controlled, composed. He sips his water, placing the glass quietly on the stool in front of him.

We sit in silence.

Alex meets my eyes and gives a slow, knowing nod. I nod back. I let go of Scarlett's hand, rise from my seat, and embrace Alfred, a long, quiet hug. We hold it for over thirty seconds, saying nothing.

When we part, Aurelia enters to announce the food is ready.

The dining room is lavish, with a glowing fireplace, chandeliers, and a long, oval table dressed in white cloth with gold embroidery. The adjoining kitchen is clearly gourmet, with high-end appliances and a central island.

The table is a visual feast, roast beef, colourful vegetables, mashed potatoes, rich stews, nyama choma, ugali, rice, greens, kachumbari. Platters of roast potatoes and fresh salads glisten beside warm, crusty breads and soft rolls. Butters, chutneys, and creamy sauces fill porcelain bowls. Drinks include pineapple juice, orange juice, red and white wines, whiskey, and sparkling water.

We take our seats, Alex and Scarlett on one side, Alfred and I on the other. Allegra and Aurelia join us. Alfred asks us to hold hands around the table.

He begins a prayer.

"Lord, we thank you for this food and for bringing my son safely home. You are our shield, our protector. Bless the hungry and the suffering. May we always remain in Your grace. In the mighty name of Jesus Christ, we pray. Amen."

We all echo, "Amen."

Alfred smiles and nods. "Joe, please serve yourself first."

With a grin, I reach for the roast beef, my appetite and heart full.

CHAPTER THIRTY

Samuel was not a very happy man as he sat in his corner booth office and looked at the pile of paperwork awaiting him. Today was Friday, and he had no intention of going to the same place as he had the week before. He couldn't stand being around such unscrupulous individuals who treated their fellow human beings like dirt. Especially Marcus. He hated, and more than detested, that man. The man had no moral compass. He would sell his mother to the highest bidder if he could. Marcus was capable of anything, whatever he thought he could get away with.

He had made a few enemies because of his hot temper, and Samuel often thought that Marcus opened his mouth before engaging his brain, but had never said so aloud. The man was crazy and sometimes saw enemies where there were none. Samuel knew the reason Marcus kept bodyguards on his small estate, what he liked to call a "mansion" (mansion, God give me strength, mused Samuel), was because he'd upset the wrong people. These days, Marcus barely dared to venture beyond his gates. Samuel liked it that way, unlike the old days when Marcus would show up unannounced at his office, full of crazy ideas and disrupting his routine.

Samuel liked his solitude. He lived alone on the west side of the city after his wife had run off with the gardener, who doubled up as an electrician, plumber, roofer, and self-proclaimed chef. Samuel had never bothered to test those culinary skills; he detested the man instantly. He'd been proven right when the said gardener also became his wife's new husband. They had run off to live in a commune somewhere in the middle of God knew where.

Samuel was, in truth, glad to see her go. In their later years together, Wendy had not stopped yammering on about relocating to Kenya, their country of birth. They had no children, and Samuel was thrilled she had not managed to bring a child into the world. That was the one mercy she'd ever granted him.

"Don't get me wrong," Samuel thought to himself, clicking aimlessly at an overdue invoice. "I used to love her." But years of constant bickering and trying to keep up with the Joneses had worn him down. Eventually, he'd stopped caring about what Wendy got up to.

He could hardly remember the name of the man she ran off with. He did remember the night she left, though. He came home from the pub, blind drunk, to find the bitch gone. Not just gone, she'd taken everything. The bed, fridge, cooker, kettle, washing machine, furniture, TV, computer… the only thing she'd left behind was the microwave.

"Maybe she felt a tinge of guilt," he had muttered bitterly. "Left the microwave so I could warm my meals. Meals cooked where? Served on what, bitch?" She had taken all the cutlery, pots, pans, cups, and china too. Samuel figured she left the microwave behind because there wasn't space to carry it.

That Friday night, he passed out in the bathtub, not by choice. He had stumbled in, managed to lock the door, didn't turn on the lights (not wanting to wake the bitch in his drunken haze), made his way to the bathroom, pissed in the bin thinking it was the toilet, and while fumbling with his zipper, toppled backward into the tub and blacked out.

He came to around noon on Saturday, groggy and disoriented. Wandering around the house in a stupor, he couldn't believe what he was seeing. He called the police to report a burglary, and to lodge a missing person's report, because apparently the bastards had taken his wife too.

When the police arrived, they found a note in the kitchen, addressed to "Sam" from his "long-suffering wife Wendy." She was leaving to live with "a real man who can fix all the things you couldn't." And don't bother looking for me, your loser.

The police had considered charging him with wasting their time.

That incident sobered Samuel up, for a while.

It was around that time he met Marcus on a car auction site. Marcus came off as a well-to-do man. They had a few beers, and soon that became a weekly theme. Marcus began inviting Samuel to his house in the southeast of the city. Samuel quickly saw how Marcus liked to big himself up and assert dominance over everyone.

Samuel had been born in Kenya, and Marcus claimed he had too, even boasted about being a big boss in a huge company there. Samuel didn't believe him for a second and took everything Marcus said with a grain of salt.

Over time, Samuel noticed several young boys living in Marcus's house. Marcus claimed they were his "nephews," but it didn't take long for Samuel to realise they were being used for all sorts of illegal activities. Drugs. Break-ins. Theft. Marcus used them so he wouldn't get his own hands dirty.

Samuel only stayed in touch because Marcus was sometimes generous with money. And the shared birthplace in Kenya solidified their bond, at least to Marcus. At one point, Samuel even told Marcus he wanted a slice of the "pie" the boys were bringing in.

Marcus didn't like that. The idiot thought no one knew what he was up to. He warned Samuel to keep quiet, or else. Samuel had laughed behind his back, then decided to take action. He was sickened by what Marcus was doing to those boys. It was slavery. Plain and simple.

So Samuel set out to get closer to Marcus. He stopped going to his house so often. Instead, Marcus began visiting Samuel at the office. Their bond grew. Samuel paid attention. He observed.

He noticed one boy in particular: Chris. Withdrawn. Always in the library. Never allowed to leave the house without a bodyguard. Samuel made a point of speaking with him. What he heard saddened him. Chris was bright, interested in electrical engineering.

Samuel discreetly asked the bodyguards why Chris wasn't allowed out alone. They told him Chris suffered from a mental illness. Samuel didn't buy it. Chris was the sanest, most lucid person in that entire house. If anyone was unwell, it was Marcus.

Samuel detested Marcus more with every passing day. He grew closer to Chris. Brought him engineering journals. Slipped him a mobile phone. Helped him open a bank account. Even deposited money. Chris never said "thank you," but Samuel saw it in his eyes. The boy had taken to calling him "Uncle Sam" in his mind.

One day, while waiting in Marcus's study, Samuel heard shouting. He rushed out to find Marcus holding Chris in a headlock. Chris struggled to break free. It took Samuel and Jorum to separate them. Marcus seemed in a trance.

Later, Samuel learned Marcus believed Chris had sabotaged a lucrative deal. Chris was shaken. Samuel checked in on him that night. They talked. Chris confessed—it was true. He'd sabotaged the deal. He planned to keep sabotaging until Marcus let him go.

Samuel warned him, "If you push too far, he'll disappear you. You know what I mean."

They sat in silence. Then Samuel closed the door, sat beside him, and leaned in.

"I have a plan," he said quietly.

CHAPTER THIRTY-ONE

Chris was suddenly shaken awake. He opened his eyes, disoriented, and started wondering where the hell he was. He looked around and remembered that he was still on the Ethiopian Airlines flight headed for Addis Ababa. The male passenger next to him shifted his leg away from Chris's, which had inadvertently crossed into the man's seating space. Chris mumbled an apology and glanced at the watch on his right wrist. It kindly let him know they were midway through the flight and, hopefully, would be touching down in Addis Ababa Airport in about three and a half hours.

He composed himself, settled comfortably into his economy seat, and let his mind free-flow.

Chris was going to a place he had never been before, his first time flying out of England, and alone at that. He'd tried to gather as much information about Ethiopia as possible. He knew he'd struggle with the language but had been reassured that Ethiopians were quite good at spoken English, and were known to be some of the friendliest people in Africa. He had nonetheless done his homework, starting with learning about the airport he was heading to, Addis Ababa Bole International Airport, the main gateway to Ethiopia and a major hub for Ethiopian Airlines. It offered modern facilities and extensive worldwide connections.

He had a thirst for learning that he could never explain. Given his harsh upbringing, he didn't know where it came from, but he'd always found himself wanting to know more about everything. Some of his so-called mates had often joked that he had a photographic memory and started calling him "GPS" because he could read an A-to-Z map and remember it in detail. Chris never figured out how that was possible especially since some of them couldn't even read or write.

Addis Ababa Bole International Airport was located in Bole District, approximately three and a half miles southeast of Addis Ababa's city centre, serving as a vital pivot for both local and global flights.

Chris wasn't worried about transport from the airport upon landing, he already knew the plan. He knew this wouldn't have been possible a few years ago. As the plane flew steadily on its course, he looked out the port window. All he could see was darkness. His mind drifted back to a conversation he'd had with Samuel, a man of such veracity that Chris had often wondered how he ever got caught up in the nasty web Marcus spun.

Chris had affectionately come to call him Uncle Sam.

Uncle Sam had been instrumental in putting the wheels in motion that had brought Chris this far, and for that, Chris would be eternally grateful.

Chris had grown tired of the abuse and punishment from Marcus. After one incident, where Marcus blamed him for a drug deal gone wrong and put him in a headlock, Chris started plotting his exit from the "mansion." He'd grabbed a pack of twenty-four paracetamol tablets, flushed them down the toilet, tossed the empty packet on the floor, and put baking soda from the kitchen in his mouth to mimic froth.

Then he dismantled his bedroom, screaming manically in gibberish, even he didn't know what he was yelling.

He broke the mirror, the cabinet, the wardrobe, and the sink in the toilet. When Marcus arrived, followed quickly by Alphonso, Chris warded them off with a jagged piece of the broken sink. Marcus, not wanting to spill the whiskey in the tumbler in his right hand, took one look at the frothing mouth and destroyed room and shouted at Jorum, who'd also come rushing in, to "Call the police, right now, dammit!"

Chris had been taken to hospital, accompanied by Alphonso, who, acting on Marcus's orders, told staff that Chris had tried to take his own life. The empty packet of paracetamol and the chaotic scene supported the lie. Chris was admitted to a mental health ward under Section 2 of the Mental Health Act.

Section 2 allows for the detention of individuals in hospital for up to twenty-eight days for assessment and treatment of mental disorders. It's used when someone is believed to need urgent help in a hospital setting.

Chris played along, pretending that he had truly wanted to end it all, especially after the previous day when Marcus had again blamed him for sabotage and been physically aggressive. That was also the day Uncle Sam and Jorum had helped protect him. It marked a turning point in Chris's life, with Uncle Sam's help.

He remembered that day clearly. As he sat on his bed, composing himself, Uncle Sam had entered, looked outside the door, slowly closed it, and sat next to Chris.

"I have a plan," he had said.

Chris remembered every vivid detail. Uncle Sam's plan only had one flaw—it needed more time than Chris felt he had. He knew the longer he stayed under Marcus's roof, the more his mind would deteriorate. But he had one driving force that helped him bide his time.

Uncle Sam had discovered that Chris's biological parents were alive, and extremely wealthy, and that his twin brother lived in the same city. Sam had quietly started setting things in motion to get Chris away from Marcus for good.

Sam was shocked to learn the next day that Chris had "tried to take his own life" and had been sectioned. He wanted to visit him in hospital but was denied access under Marcus's orders. Sam had no choice but to carry out his plan from afar and stopped returning to Marcus's house. He was surprised, but relieved, when he heard that Chris had absconded from the hospital after just a week, with no one knowing how he'd done it.

Chris remembered every moment of that escape.

Although Alphonso was cited as the responsible guardian, and Marcus as next of kin, Chris was adamantly against being admitted. Staff believed he was a suicide risk. Two doctors—one Section 12 approved (meaning specially trained in mental health)—signed the papers. An Approved Mental Health Practitioner agreed. Chris had heard it all before. He'd been to the same hospital as an informal patient in the past, so he knew the system and the language.

He spent the first few days pretending to watch the boring TV programs in the lounge, all the while scoping out the ward, watching staff. He began planning his escape the moment he arrived. Alphonso wasn't allowed on the ward and instead rotated with another bodyguard outside in the car.

On the sixth day, Chris requested to be escorted to the local shop to buy snacks. He was given five pounds and, as luck would have it, was assigned an agency support worker he knew to be kind and empathetic. Chris felt guilty for what he was about to do, but needs must.

He'd noticed a side exit often used by staff escorting patients to gardening sessions. It was far from the main entrance, where Alphonso usually parked. He suggested they take that route, said he wanted to check out the gardens, claiming he loved gardening (a lie, of course). The staff member happily agreed, sharing that she and her husband had an allotment and loved growing things. She was surprised, Chris usually read books about engines.

They left through the side exit. Once they'd admired the garden (which bored Chris senseless), they cleared the hospital grounds. Chris turned to her and said quietly, "I'm sorry. I have to do this," and ran.

She stood frozen, knowing she'd be in trouble. Patients weren't supposed to use that exit without supervision. She watched until Chris disappeared, then returned to the ward to follow procedure for an absconded patient.

Chris, for the first time, felt truly free. He knew exactly where to go. The hospital wasn't a concern—he knew patients on longer sections who'd absconded and never been brought back. His only focus was avoiding Marcus, and contacting Sam.

He knew Marcus's territory in the southeast was off-limits, but he smiled at the thought of Alphonso still sitting in that car, clueless.

Back when he was living rough, Chris had found a large, disused warehouse and had often taken refuge there. He converted two rooms into a makeshift base, crashing there when he didn't want to be found. He'd discovered a disused generator nearby and, using his limited electrical know-how, rigged up a power system so complex that real experts would have scratched their heads.

The warehouse, located on the city's south side, was a decaying relic, crumbling brick walls, spider webbed cracks, missing windows, moss on exposed timber, sagging roof, and thick air heavy with damp and decay. But Chris wasn't fazed. He'd seen worse—and this place had purpose.

He used the five pounds to buy a takeaway meal and slept in his hideout. The next day, he planned to retrieve his passport, mobile phone, and bank card from Marcus's house. Clothes didn't matter.

He'd made himself comfortable, rigging a hammock, bringing in an air mattress and bed covers. He was good at what he called "resource reallocation", not stealing, as he'd joke. With his street smarts and money earned from past crimes, he'd bought second-hand items: a mini fridge-freezer, a hob, a microwave that beeped obnoxiously, a kettle, and a PlayStation 5 stolen during a burglary.

His prize possession? A full computer setup with three monitors, stolen from the home of a city trader. He set it up like a miniature communications hub—his love for electronics shining through. His mates never understood why he didn't just pawn the gear.

A swivel chair rounded out the setup.

A sudden jolt from turbulence snapped Chris back to the present. The seatbelt signs came on. The pilot's calm voice reassured passengers that they were passing through "a bit of rough weather." Flight crew walked the aisles, calming nerves.

Chris took a deep gulp of sparkling water, leaned back into his seat, and waited for the shaking to pass.

CHAPTER THIRTY-TWO

"What do you mean he has escaped?!!" Marcus thundered, glaring at Alphonso, who stood sheepishly in the living room with his hands by his sides.

"It's a damn hospital ward and he was on a section 2!!" Marcus shouted, foam forming at the corners of his mouth.

Alphonso simply stood there. He'd followed instructions: stay in the car park and watch if Chris ever left the ward. Even if with staff, he was to follow him. Entering the ward was strictly prohibited by hospital policy. What had Marcus expected him to do?

Marcus paced up and down the room. Alphonso didn't feel the slightest sympathy for him. He was getting tired of Marcus, his arrogance, the way he treated everyone like they were beneath him. Ever since Chris had come to live there, Marcus had been muttering about "getting back What's rightfully mine" and "atonement day." Alphonso had seen two men regularly visiting Marcus, always retreating into the study for hushed discussions. One of them, Samuel, had taken a liking to Chris. They'd formed a quiet bond Marcus remained oblivious to. Alphonso, in truth, was glad Chris had escaped. He suspected Marcus was planning something nefarious.

Marcus had taken the loss badly. He spent days locked in his study, glued to his phone or computer. Of the two men who used to visit, only Samuel had stopped coming, though Alphonso didn't dare ask Marcus why.

Ten days after Chris went missing, Marcus summoned his four bodyguards into the study. They were ordered to comb through every known place Chris had been—former foster homes, street connections, no stone was to be left unturned.

Even Marcus's "nephews" were drafted into the search. Teenagers who could move unnoticed where the bulky bodyguards couldn't. Marcus promised big rewards if they found Chris, even handed out wads of cash to motivate them. But after a week, the trail had gone cold.

Marcus grew desperate. He kept eyeing the calendar, panicked by time slipping away. Finally, in a last-ditch effort, he made a phone call, speaking for over half an hour before hanging up with the words, "I'll see you first thing tomorrow morning."

The red brick building on St. James Street loomed ahead as Alphonso parked the black Toyota Avensis in a spot clearly marked NO PARKING AT ANY TIME. He opened the back door and Marcus stepped out, dressed in what he considered a smart blue suit, white shirt, and black tie. He straightened himself, unbuttoned his coat. His sixty years showed plainly on his face, disappointment, failure, though he tried to look upbeat.

People's essence is often revealed in posture, speech, and expression. Some crave love to escape their emotional enclosures. Others need understanding for healthy mental and emotional development. From their attitudes, we adjust ours. But Marcus fit neither mold. He was a man used to bulldozing through life, with no regard for others.

Inside the building, they approached the reception desk where a blonde woman sat on the phone. She gestured for them to take a seat.

Alphonso noted the tidy surroundings, unlike Marcus's chaotic study. A brown leather sofa sat beside a bookcase. A dark mahogany table stood nearby. A water cooler occupied a corner. The receptionist, strikingly beautiful, had snow-white skin, sky-blue eyes, bright red lipstick, and an ethereal presence. She asked, "May I help you, gentlemen?"

Marcus, puffing up with self-importance, said he was there to see Mr. Atkins.

Just then, the bronze door beside the desk swung open. A man appeared and said, "It's okay, Sophie," then beckoned them in.

Marcus walked through without a handshake. Alphonso stayed behind, lounged on the plush sofa, and pulled out his phone, ignoring Sophie.

Inside, Marcus took a seat across from a polished wooden desk. The man who'd opened the door stood silently, examining Marcus. Around them, the room was decorated with wildlife art—a bronzed wildebeest head hung beside the desk.

"I'm here at last," Marcus said, fidgeting. "We've spoken before. No need for formalities."

"Marcus," the man said, finally sitting. His blue eyes held a trace of amusement. He smiled, showing perfect white teeth. "I finally get to meet you."

"Finally, Atkins," Marcus replied with disdain. "I wouldn't have left my humble abode if this wasn't important. It had to be face-to-face."

"I don't blame you," said Atkins, leaning back in his swivel chair. "Your boy ran off, and now you're desperate. You need him to claim what you think is yours."

"Exactly," Marcus said. "Help me, and you'll have a lucrative position in my company. No more running errands. I need Chris back urgently, and the rewards—well, you know."

Atkins studied him. "The only reason I kept contact with you was Francis—who, by the way, was shot by your goons and survived. You didn't send a card. Didn't visit. Just used him to clean up your messes."

He continued, "Joe, who knew nothing about Chris, knows now. He knows everything. He's with his real family in Mtwapa, and I know That's eating you alive."

Atkins leaned forward. "Francis gave me something before he disappeared. When Joe brought it, I knew: the only one I'd help was Chris. But you'd never let him go, would you?"

"I've heard what goes on in your so-called mansion," Atkins said. "I wonder how Chris will feel when he finds out who you really are."

He stood. "I don't want you in my office anymore."

Marcus, clearly desperate, reached into his coat and produced a brown envelope. He placed it on the desk.

"There's fifteen grand in there," he said. "More to come if you help bring Chris back. You'll have your pick of roles in my company, including positions abroad."

Atkins walked around the desk, took the envelope, and shoved it into Marcus's chest.

"You're a man without morals," he said coldly. "You exploit everyone. You took advantage of Francis, of those teenage boys. You turned them into drug dealers in exchange for a roof over their heads. You beat them into silence."

He paced. "You call it a mansion? It's just an overcrowded HMO. Francis told me everything. He was going to blackmail you. That envelope—proof of your crimes. Despite your drug money, you do nothing to better their lives. You probably feed them drugs just to keep them around."

He turned to Marcus. "I'm glad Chris escaped. If he's smart, he's telling the police everything. I wonder how he'll feel when he learns you and Alfred are half-brothers."

"Get out of my office. I never want to see you again."

Marcus left without a word.

CHAPTER THIRTY-THREE

Chris had not been singing like a canary to the police as he had just spent the entire morning mapping out the way that he was going to move forward. He had come up with an inventory of the things that he wanted to acquire for himself, and he knew exactly how he was going to get them. He didn't need to write anything down; his memory was sufficient.

He'd used the change left over from last night's takeaway to place a phone call to Samuel, who had been thrilled to hear from him and had immediately wanted to know where he was.

"I'm afraid I can't tell you that, Uncle Sam," Chris had said, speaking from a British Telecommunications call box on Vauxhall Street, about a mile from his hideout in the disused warehouse. "Just in case Marcus has put a tail on you, thinking I might meet you for help. Though I don't think he's that bright, and he certainly hasn't got the resources for something like that."

"I want to help you," Samuel had replied. "And it's a good thing I've been depositing money for you. You can get far away from Marcus; to a place he'll never find you. Remember what we talked about in your bedroom that day?"

Chris had remembered very well. Samuel had pitched the idea of springing him out of Marcus's grasp and helping him leave the country.

"Where to?" Chris had asked.

"Don't you see?" Samuel had said. "Marcus is keeping you around so he can use you as leverage against Alfred, so he can take over his vast business empire. There are rumours. Marcus can't keep his mouth shut, especially when he's drunk. Alfred—your biological father, doesn't have long to live. Neither does your mother. Apparently, she has breast cancer. Marcus is Alfred's half-brother. Same father, different mothers."

Chris had furrowed his brow. He had felt as if he were choking. Half-brother by blood?! The way Marcus treated him!

Seeing Chris's anger rising, Samuel had continued, "Marcus used to be part of Alfred's business empire, but he was as unscrupulous then as he is now. He thought the company should be run 50/50. But Alfred and his wife, your mother, started it. Alfred only put Marcus on the board out of pity. As the business grew, Marcus grew more jealous. He thought he was entitled to more than what he got.

"Alfred had political ambitions. He entertained high-powered government officials at his huge villa in Muthaiga North Springs Estate, just over seven miles from the city centre."

Chris had sat there in disbelief, his fists clenched. He had signalled for Samuel to go on.

"Marcus, out of jealousy and spite, met with criminal investigation officials and told them Alfred and his associates were plotting a coup. With help from bribed contacts, using Alfred's own money, he produced fake documents. He convinced them to bug him, claiming he could lure Alfred into revealing the plan.

"But Marcus leaked his intentions to confidants, promising them big stakes in the company. One of them was a source Alfred trusted. He tipped Alfred off. Alfred, knowing how the regime operated, plotted his escape. His wife Kathleen was pregnant at the time. They fled to England. She gave birth to twins, James and Joshua. Chris was James. He was born five minutes before his brother."

Chris had felt as if he were dreaming. James and Joshua!

There'd been a break in the conversation when Marcus came to check on what was taking Samuel so long to console Chris. Samuel had convinced him to get a drink and promised to join him in twenty minutes. He'd returned to Chris and picked up where he left off.

Samuel explained that Alfred had cut communication with the company after three-quarters of the board had been arrested on trumped-up charges. He'd gone into hiding. Meanwhile, Marcus assumed the role of chairman and CEO. Alfred despaired, knowing the empire he'd built was doomed under Marcus.

He and Kathleen had hired a nanny and cook in England. The anger they felt dissipated each morning they looked at their sons. They thanked God for blessing them.

Chris had stood and begun pacing. He wanted to confront Marcus. But Samuel had calmed him.

Samuel glanced at his watch. Only five minutes left before Marcus got suspicious. But he knew Marcus would be too drunk to care.

Apparently, when the twins were a few months old, masked men had broken into the house, kidnapping Alfred and Kathleen and leaving the twins alone. The nanny called the police. James and Joshua ended up with different foster parents.

Samuel added that Alfred and Kathleen were held in their home country for two years before being released. Alfred vanished, operating from the shadows, using his wealth to trace his sons and bring those responsible to justice.

Samuel said Marcus had once drunkenly admitted that Alfred was obsessed with finding his children, pouring all his resources into it.

Just then, Marcus knocked again, and Samuel stood up, winking at Chris before leaving.

After that, Chris had refused dinner. He stayed in his room, lost in thought, plotting his escape.

"Are you still there?" Samuel's voice echoed through the earpiece, snapping him back to the present.

"Yes, sorry, Uncle Sam," Chris replied.

"Can I meet you at a place of your choosing? I know Marcus and his goons are looking for you. But you can't let him near you."

They agreed to meet somewhere Marcus would never think to go: outside the Mandarin Oriental Hyde Park in Knightsbridge.

Samuel had wondered how Chris knew of the Mandarin Oriental. He'd looked it up online after hanging up, relieved the meeting wasn't inside, his wallet wouldn't survive. He admired Chris's cleverness.

Four hours later, Chris was back in his hideout with everything Samuel had gotten him. He sat in front of his computer screens, devouring fried chicken and orange juice, clicking away.

Samuel had bought him a burner phone, now charging beside his left monitor. Chris mentally ticked off his inventory: two silver suitcases (large and small), formal clothes, hot-weather clothes, sandals, socks, innerwear, t-shirts, beachwear, sunglasses, sunscreen, insect repellent. The suitcases were beside his air mattress, along with blue sandals, black shoes, and dark tan ones. A black suit hung near the hammock. He also had a holdall.

Satisfied, he returned to the computer, focusing on a city map displayed on the central screen. After a careful review, he dressed in his suit and black leather shoes, took some banknotes, pocketed the burner phone, and quietly exited the warehouse.

The building beside the disused warehouse was a Travelodge Hotel, and its high fence hid the warehouse from sight. Chris thanked his lucky stars daily for being able to use the Travelodge Wi-Fi through his PlayStation 5.

He made his way to his destination, climbed to the first floor, ignoring the creaky elevator, and walked to the flat he was targeting. The blinds were drawn shut. He stood quietly, then tested the brown door, it was locked. The recessed doorway concealed him from view.

He pretended to fumble for keys, then peeked down the corridor—only to come face-to-face with two women. One wore a black flowing dress, red auburn hair, and sandals. The other had on blue jeans, a white tank top, and white trainers. Her black hair was in a ponytail, and her piercing ebony eyes studied Chris.

"Hello, can we help you?" the one with the ponytail asked.

Chris hesitated. He hadn't expected anyone.

Adjusting his dark glasses, he calmly reached into his holdall, pulled out four £20 notes, and handed two to each woman.

"Tell anyone who asks that you didn't see me," he said.

Then he turned, descended the stairs, and disappeared from sight—leaving the two women outside the flat, probably wondering what on earth had just happened.

CHAPTER THIRTY-FOUR

After the sumptuous meal, we all retire to the living room and Alfred disappears somewhere. The mood is relaxed, although Scarlett and I can now feel the effects of the long journey. It's almost ten o'clock at night, and the dreaded jet lag is setting in. As if reading my thoughts, Alfred suddenly reappears and announces that he's going to show us to our bedrooms so we can unwind and perhaps take a shower, an idea Scarlett and I both welcome.

Alex has resumed his spot in the chair he occupied earlier, gleefully nursing another fresh glass of Macallan while scrolling through his phone.

Alfred leads us through the main hallway adjacent to the entrance, and I can't stop marvelling at the place. He guides us up a bronze staircase into another hallway. We pass a few massive rooms, each more beautiful than the last. The place is unparalleled.

He opens a door and gestures for us to enter. I marvel at the beauty of the room.

It's massive, with a king-size bed at its centre, adorned with shimmering red satin sheets. A huge television is mounted on the adjacent wall, flanked by surround speakers. Below it sits a white bookcase, filled with a myriad of books. The Hilton doesn't begin to compare to this.

Scarlett draws a sharp breath as we move around, taking it all in. There are silver bedside cabinets on either side of the bed and golden table lamps that make the entire bed space look majestic. The headboard is a curved mirror decorated with roses, enough to make anyone stop and simply stare, which is exactly what we're doing.

Alfred points toward the ensuite bathroom. As Scarlett steps in, her breath is taken away. It's a bathroom, yes, but one fit for royalty. My tiny flat's bathroom could easily fit inside this one.

Golden taps gleam on a huge sunken bathtub. Everywhere I look is a celebration of white and beige. There's a toilet, a massive sink with golden taps, a bidet, and a wet room with a walk-in shower. On one wall stands a magnificent cabinet with floor-to-ceiling glass doors, framed with golden handles. Inside, There's an array of ointments, soaps, aftershaves, men's and women's perfumes, toothbrushes, and toothpaste. This bathroom screams luxury.

We return to the bedroom, and Alfred shows us a huge walk-in closet. One side is filled with drawers, and I'm surprised to find all the clothes we brought from England neatly hung up. Additional clothes have been provided, along with extra bedsheets and covers. Scarlett's eyes widen, she loves clothes. Alfred must run this household like clockwork. We hadn't even noticed our luggage arriving from the airport.

There are suits, ties, trousers, long- and short-sleeve shirts… I feel like I've stepped into a boutique.

As if on cue, I glance toward where the mini-office would have been at the Hilton. Scarlett and I exchange glances.

We leave the closet and sit down on two plush red velvet sofas, still absorbing the splendour around us. The room's layout is completed by a computer desk with a desktop computer, a marble telephone, and several chests of drawers with bronze handles.

Alfred tells us to rest and to come downstairs if we need anything—he understands how exhausting the journey has been. Then he quietly takes his leave.

Scarlett and I look at each other. We're so tired we barely think about showering. We've seen nightclothes in the closet, so we freshen up, and within twenty minutes, we're both fast asleep.

I wake up first. I move gently, not wanting to disturb Scarlett. I always admire her when she sleeps, she looks so peaceful.

This time, I don't have to retreat to a mini-office to process Alex's information. I'm at the heart of it all now.

I take a long, warm shower and get dressed in khaki shorts, a loose white T-shirt, and brown sandals. Heading downstairs via the bronze staircase, I still can't get enough of this place.

I find Alfred reading some papers in the dining room. As soon as he sees me, he stands, folds the papers neatly, and sets them aside. He's smartly dressed in a blue suit and matching shirt—no tie. His black leather shoes shine.

He embraces me warmly.

"Good morning, Joe," he says, pulling out a chair for me.

"Good morning," I reply, sitting down. Alfred returns to his seat.

He asks if I'd like breakfast or prefer to wait for Scarlett. As I study him, I notice his eyes seem sunken. I wonder what kind of life he's lived to get where he is today.

I tell him breakfast can wait. I ask him to tell me about his life, and when we might go visit Kathleen. I'd really love to meet her.

He asks me to walk with him.

We navigate a maze of brightly lit hallways and arrive at what appears to be his study. He punches a code into a keypad beside a bronze door, then opens it.

This must be his inner sanctum, and I'm right.

It's a plush office furnished with expensive-looking sofas. A massive glass table stands atop a white Persian rug. The whole space exudes peace and comfort.

Against one wall sits a huge mahogany desk with one of the most comfortable-looking leather chairs I've ever seen. For some reason, I long to sit behind it.

The carpet is thick and blue. Numerous pictures hang on the walls. While Alfred moves to a fridge across the room, I barely notice. My attention is caught by several photographs of identical babies.

There are hospital photos, new-borns with Alfred and a woman I don't immediately recognise. But as I look closer, I realise it must be Kathleen—my biological mother— holding the two babies with a radiant smile.

I don't move. I barely notice that Alfred is now standing beside me, watching as I study the photographs.

Other pictures show the proud parents leaving the hospital and arriving at what must have been the babies" first home. The twins look identical. It must've been nearly impossible to tell them apart at that age.

Still, Alfred says nothing.

Then my eyes land on a portrait of Kathleen, clearly taken before she gave birth. She's stunning. Fine features. A well-shaped nose. Wavy black hair. Sincere brown eyes. And that smile, the proudest I've ever seen.

I can't take my eyes off the portrait. She seems to be looking directly at me, smiling. I feel a swell of pride and reach out, gently brushing her face through the glass.

There are more pictures, Alfred in business meetings, Kathleen at home, in parks, outside a church, but none of the twins as they grew older.

Now I understand what Alex meant when he said our biological parents were abducted when we were just months old. Somehow, Alfred managed to preserve these few photos. I plan to ask him how.

I finally turn. Alfred gestures for me to sit on one of the sofas. He sits across from me. On the table between us, he places a pitcher of orange juice and two glasses. He pours for both of us and hands me one.

He leans back, relaxes, and begins.

"It all started quite a long time ago," Alfred says, taking a sip from his glass.

CHAPTER THIRTY-FIVE

The Ethiopian Airlines flight from London Gatwick touched down at Addis Ababa Bole International Airport at exactly six in the evening, local time. Chris waited patiently as the disembarking passengers chatted animatedly in languages he couldn't understand. In preparation for the flight, he had found out that Ethiopia's official languages were Amharic, Somali, Oromo, Tigrigna, and Afar, though English was also widely spoken, which reassured him that he wouldn't struggle too much with the language barrier.

After exiting the plane, Chris knew he didn't need to go through immigration and baggage claim, as he was in transit and his luggage had been checked through to his final destination. He needed to catch a connecting flight, according to the itinerary Uncle Sam had worked out for him, so he followed the transit signs and passed through security checks, heading for departures.

He checked his tickets again and saw that flight 724, his connecting flight, would be leaving in five hours. It would take two hours and roughly forty-five minutes. He wasn't bothered by the wait; he was in no particular hurry, taking this journey one step at a time. The airport was quite large, he noticed, and surprisingly modern. He wandered around, dragging his carry-on luggage, admiring the sleek architecture, the polished interior design, and, most notably, he saw that the Wi-Fi was free.

There were signs for gift shops, duty-free stores, and a coffee lounge, and he decided to stop and get himself a coffee and something to eat. He connected his burner phone to the free Wi-Fi and settled in a corner with his coffee and a snack. Logging in, he started reading the news, he always liked to keep up with what was happening around the world, especially anything related to engineering. He liked this airport, even though it was the first time he had actually flown. He liked the ambiance, the soft hue of the lighting, the smell in the air, and, most importantly to him, the beautiful, alluring, sexy Ethiopian women.

As Chris admired the women and sipped his coffee while surfing the web, his uncle Sam was on a bus from Nairobi to Mombasa. After buying everything Chris needed, Samuel had finalised the travel arrangements. Since Chris hadn't wanted to reveal where he was staying, Sam had said he would visit Marcus one last time. Chris had told him that his passport was still in his old bedroom at Marcus's house, locked in a small safe for which he alone had the code. Chris had given that code to Uncle Sam, who had stated he wouldn't go into the bedroom himself to avoid raising Marcus's suspicions, especially as rumours were already spreading that Samuel might be hiding Chris somewhere. Extra precaution was necessary.

Uncle Sam had instead decided to give the code to Jorum. He already had Jorum's number, and the burner phone would be untraceable. Samuel had remarked that Marcus would never suspect Jorum, not in a million years, and that he was the perfect person to deliver Chris's passport, especially during his regular running routine. What Samuel found amazing was that Chris could remember his entire passport number and every single detail about it, he hadn't anticipated Chris's photographic memory.

That was how he had been able to buy the Ethiopian Airlines ticket. Samuel had avoided booking a direct flight to Nairobi, he wasn't taking any chances.

The itinerary was that Chris would catch a connecting flight to Mombasa, and the timing had been arranged so that Samuel would arrive in Mombasa before him and meet him at the airport. Samuel had gathered enough public information about Alfred and his massive CODENIENIS empire, with head offices in Nairobi and branches across the country. Alfred Keynudhia, it seemed, was a shy man who avoided the limelight. Very little was known about his private life. Samuel found it difficult to believe that Alfred and Marcus were related, they were like chalk and cheese, judging from Alfred's scarce public profile.

Samuel was also aware that Chris's twin brother, Joe, was already in Mtwapa, the sprawling estate featured in several magazines, where Alfred liked to spend most of his time. Marcus had given up trying to snatch Joe. Joe had bodyguards that even Marcus and his crew couldn't see, but they were always there. Marcus, with his inept spies, knew Joe had left the country to reunite with his biological parents.

Samuel had given Jorum the code to the small safe under the bed in Chris's former bedroom. Chris had arranged a rendezvous where Jorum delivered the passport, airline tickets, and some money. Jorum had done it all for free, he'd grown tired of Marcus's put-downs and the toxic atmosphere, especially around Alphonso. Jorum had grown increasingly uneasy, especially after Chris ran off from the support worker at the hospital. Marcus's paranoia had spiralled; he'd bought two German Alsatian dogs that he now let loose on the property at all times.

Jorum had been glad, more than happy, to help Chris. He knew Chris hadn't been treated fairly.

Samuel checked the time on his watch. The journey was taking seven and a half hours, and he was almost there. By his calculations, Chris would soon be enroute to Moi International Airport. He leaned back in his seat and drifted off. The bus moved along at a sedate pace. Everyone else was silent, with almost three-quarters of the passengers either asleep or trying to fall asleep.

As all this was taking place, Chris waiting for his connecting flight, Samuel nearing Mombasa by bus, I was seated in the dining room with Scarlett, Alfred, and Alex. A few papers were scattered on the table, and a black briefcase lay open by Alfred's side. Alex was sipping still water, ice cubes clinking softly in his glass, while he typed on a silver Surf-Pro laptop. Scarlett had settled for a cup of tea, and I was drinking orange juice. I like orange juice.

Alfred, wearing black reading glasses, was deep in thought, silver pen in hand as he perused the papers. Scarlett and I chatted in low tones.

The day had passed quickly for us, and Alfred had shared a great deal of information—most of which, though not all, echoed what Alex had already told me. Still, it was incredible to hear it from the horse's mouth, so to speak. Alfred had told me he was an only child raised by his mother, Emily. His father had not been a consistent part of their lives. Born with a natural flair for business, Alfred had excelled at school and graduated university with a first-class honours degree in business.

He began working in the property market, managing properties for a major housing company. It was around this time that he met Kathleen, his future wife. They fell in love, got married, and settled in a nice estate in Nairobi. Kathleen came from an affluent family and had never lacked anything. What Alfred loved most about her was her kind heart and generosity.

Then he told me something that made the hairs on the back of my neck stand on end: he had a half-brother named Marcus. I recalled all the unsettling things Alex had said about Marcus.

Alfred and Kathleen had started investing in run-down properties using an inheritance Kathleen had received from her father, a sharp-witted wheeler-dealer. They renovated and resold the properties at a profit. The market was booming, and it had been the perfect time to invest. Before long, they expanded into renovating office buildings, and within a few years, they'd built an impressive business portfolio. They bought a four-bedroom house for themselves and began to enjoy the fruits of their labour.

I hadn't dared to interrupt Alfred as he refilled our drinks and resumed the story. I was captivated.

What really hooked me was Marcus being Alfred's half-brother. Alfred had a commanding presence when he spoke, the kind that held your attention.

Their success led to the opening of a headquarters in the capital. Over time, they diversified into manufacturing and farming, coffee, tea, pyrethrum, cotton, flowers. The company had evolved into a powerful entity. Alfred said he was content and had stayed in touch with Marcus, even inviting him over for dinners. But Kathleen had never liked him, she was a good judge of character and had always been diligent in her work with Alfred.

Out of pity, Alfred had given Marcus a role in the company. He also gifted him a three-bedroom house. Initially, things went smoothly. Alfred had even begun considering a run for Parliament and had begun networking with influential government officials, hosting them in the mansion he'd gifted Kathleen in the upscale Muthaiga North Springs estate. Marcus was rarely invited. Kathleen had sensed Marcus's resentment and warned Alfred to be careful.

Alfred hadn't invited Marcus to these high-level events because Marcus drank too much and often made a fool of himself. Jealousy consumed him, jealous of Alfred's success, bitter toward Kathleen. Reports started surfacing of Marcus bullying junior executives, often hiding behind his brother's name and threatening them with dismissal. Alarmed, Alfred had him transferred multiple times, eventually relocating him to Changamwe to oversee an oil refinery.

Changamwe was nearly 300 kilometres from Nairobi, and Alfred had instructed the management there to report Marcus's behaviour directly to him.

At this point, Alfred paused the story and requested a late breakfast, more like brunch, and I was pleased that Scarlett had been able to join us just then.

CHAPTER THIRTY-SIX

Scarlett had been dressed in a white sari-style dress, cinched at the waist with a black belt. She wore brown sandals and looked every bit the beauty she was, lending the room an air of graceful, heralded elegance.

The food had been delicious: fried eggs, toast with butter and jam, boiled and poached eggs, pancakes with maple syrup and honey, a choice of cereals and porridge, along with tea, coffee, and a selection of juices. I had chosen coffee, fried eggs, toast with jam, and finished it off with a cold glass of orange juice. Scarlett had gone for tea and pancakes (as I knew she would), along with a poached egg and a bowl of cereal. Alfred had settled for juice and a poached egg, stating he wasn't very hungry.

After we had finished eating, Alfred continued with his story, this time with Scarlett snuggled up beside me. She couldn't wait to hear what he had to say. I had told her I'd fill her in on everything she had missed, and she had smiled that one-million-watt smile of hers.

Alfred began by saying that I had been born 21 years ago and was part of a pair of identical twins. During Kathleen's pregnancy with my twin brother and me, they had been forced to flee the country and seek refuge in England, where we had apparently been born. They had settled in the suburbs of an idyllic town, and Alfred had tried to stay in touch with his business associates, most of whom had been rounded up and detained. He'd caught wind that his business had been taken over and that people were actively hunting him, so he avoided all contact with anyone connected to his past.

Then came the shock: when we were just a few months old, masked men broke into our family home and kidnapped our parents, leaving us alone. It was the nanny who had alerted the police, and once authorities arrived, we were placed in separate foster homes.

Alfred continued. After nearly two years of captivity, he and Kathleen were somehow freed. They went into hiding, determined to restructure and reclaim what they had built from scratch. Alfred revealed he had hidden away substantial funds in offshore accounts and began operating silently, hell-bent on bringing those responsible to justice. Vengeance, he admitted, was in his blood.

He had made every effort to trace my twin brother and me, using his wealth and network of contacts. Eventually, he discovered where I had been fostered and later adopted by the couple who raised me. But he hadn't been able to find Chris. That search, he said, was still ongoing.

Then came the betrayal, he had found out that it was Marcus who had betrayed him. After Alfred reclaimed control of his company, Marcus vanished from the country, taking a substantial chunk of the company's finances with him.

Despite the heavy content, Alfred's voice lightened slightly as he recounted the steps he'd taken to rebuild his empire. Still, I noticed he was beginning to tire. It had clearly been a long journey to get to this point, and telling the story was wearing on him.

He told us that Kathleen—my biological mother—had developed breast cancer and was now in the final stages of her illness. She was in a hospice not far from the estate, and we would soon be able to visit her.

Then Alfred revealed something that left me speechless: he too was ill. He had been diagnosed with heart failure, and his doctors had given him approximately four years to live. He said it was time to get his affairs in order.

Alfred said he wanted to hand over control of the business to his sons, and since I was the one present, thanks to Alex, he would be holding a board meeting to announce the change. He explained that he would go over the most important business matters with me and his most trusted associates, and then he asked me how I felt about all of it.

I was stunned. He was also dying.

What I wanted most at that moment was to hug him, and to see Kathleen.

A business empire? Oh my.

Alfred then explained the process of transferring ownership. It involved legal and financial steps, preparing share transfer forms, updating company records, and potentially consulting legal and financial advisors. Fortunately, his team had already handled most of this. Since Alfred was the sole owner, the transfer wouldn't require selling assets or creating a new business entity. He spoke about business lawyers and legal compliance requirements; terms I was barely familiar with. But once again, he assured me everything had been reviewed and put in place by his accountants, and we'd go over the final details in the coming days.

He hinted that he would mentor me through the transition and help me develop a timeline to take on the responsibilities.

I was truly amazed. Scarlett squeezed my arm as Alfred continued. I remembered what Alex had told me: if everything went according to plan, I'd never have to work again.

Incredible.

Alfred noticed that I seemed overwhelmed. He softened his tone and spoke with a warmer, more fatherly cadence. He asked me not to dwell too much on everything just yet. But how could I not?

He added that, post-transfer, he would serve as an advisor, using the time he had left to ensure everything ran smoothly. I was at a loss for words. The scope of this company, this legacy, was mind-boggling.

I didn't have a head for business, but I was good at budgeting and instinctive risk-taking, whatever that meant to me at the time.

We spent more time chatting. Scarlett shared stories about her parents (which Alfred already knew from Alex's briefings) and how they had emigrated to England and raised a loving family. She was especially taken by the luxurious décor of the estate's study and had fallen in love with the colour palette.

At the dining table, Alfred was still studying some papers. I turned to Scarlett and suggested we explore the house. I asked Alfred if that would be alright.

"Of course, by all means," he replied, looking up. "Soon, all this will be yours, so feel right at home."

He began placing the papers back into his black briefcase. I noticed Alex hadn't said much since we arrived the day before. I respected that, he was giving me time to get to know Alfred on my own terms. I was also surprised he hadn't reached for his Macallan, but I guessed he was busy checking in with his private investigators back in England.

Scarlett and I held hands and strolled down the hallway leading from the dining room. The cream-coloured walls were pristine. As we passed by tall windows, we could see grand ocean views. This place, which could one day be mine, was opulent beyond anything I had ever imagined.

We stepped outside into the warm night, a soft breeze on our faces. The sky was studded with stars, and the gentle sound of waves filled the air. The estate sprawled luxuriously. In the distance, we could see a well-lit private beach and a stunning infinity pool. I was tempted to take a dip.

As we stood in awe, Scarlett rested her head on my shoulder. "This is paradise, my darling. I feel like I want to stay here for the rest of my life," she said, wrapping her arms around my waist. She turned and raised her lips to mine. I leaned in and kissed her. We stayed like that for a while, wrapped in each other's arms.

When we broke the kiss, we continued wandering through the illuminated estate, the grounds aglow in soft hues of blue, lilac, and crimson, lights that seemed to emanate from the perfectly manicured lawns. It felt magical.

Unbeknownst to us, guards were patrolling the perimeter. Each one, we would later discover, had their own trained dog, among the most elite security dogs in the world. A long, winding driveway led to what I assumed was the main gate, and nestled among the lush greenery was what looked like a guardhouse. We didn't go that way, we simply stood there, soaking in the tranquillity.

Back inside, we passed the dining room again. Alfred and Alex were deep in conversation, so we continued our self-guided tour. We entered a spacious living room with floor-to-ceiling windows, cosy seating, and a grand fireplace.

Scarlett suggested we check upstairs, where she had seen more beautiful rooms earlier. I agreed. Upstairs, we discovered large bedrooms, most with ensuite bathrooms and some with private balconies. There was a home theatre, a game room with a snooker table, and a fully equipped gym with a spa.

The home theatre especially caught my eye, it was built like a mini cinema, with seating for about thirty people. I wondered what movies might be in the collection, imagining the sound of the surround system echoing through the room.

Scarlett pointed out a glass cabinet near the entrance. Inside, neatly arranged, were three rows of IMAX 3D glasses.

Exhilarating!

We took two seats at the front and snuggled in, holding hands, letting the enormity of it all sink in as time passed us by.

CHAPTER THIRTY-SEVEN

Ethiopian Airlines flight 724 from Bole International Airport in Addis Ababa touched down at Moi International Airport in Mombasa at five minutes past one in the morning. Chris was wide awake. He had enjoyed the flight despite some turbulence an hour after takeoff. The pilot announced their arrival, noting the cool, breezy night, and thanked passengers for flying Ethiopian Airlines, wishing them a pleasant stay in Mombasa.

Chris waited for most passengers to collect their carry-ons before standing and retrieving his own, stepping into the slow-moving queue toward the exit. There wasn't much chatter. *Must be the time of night,* he thought.

After immigration, customs, and baggage claim, where he collected the silver suitcase Uncle Sam had bought for him, he exited into the arrivals hall, knowing Sam would be waiting, as per their itinerary.

A few hours earlier, Samuel had arrived at the airport via taxi from the Simba Coach bus stop where his journey from Nairobi had ended. With time to spare, he had checked into the hotel apartment he'd booked in advance for the two of them—a twin room offering complimentary breakfast. Not that food was a priority. He was a man on a mission.

The hotel was close to the Nguuni Nature Sanctuary, though Samuel hadn't given it much thought; what mattered was its proximity to Mtwapa, just six and a half miles away. After a quick shower to freshen up, he'd taken another taxi to the airport and now waited in the arrivals area. Dressed in army beach shorts, a loose green t-shirt, safari boots, and a grey baseball cap, Samuel spotted Chris immediately and strode toward him.

Chris, pushing his trolley, grinned and embraced his uncle. The two hugged warmly before Samuel took over the trolley.

"How was the flight?" he asked as they made their way to the exit, where a taxi waited.

Chris shrugged. "Good. Especially the stewardess service."

Samuel grinned and continued pushing the trolley. Soon, they were in the taxi, heading for the apartment. Chris stared out the window, taking in late-night Mombasa: brightly lit shopfronts, sparse foot traffic, and the city's subdued nighttime hum. Uncle Sam remained mostly quiet, estimating the ride to be just over ten miles.

At the hotel apartment, Chris declared he desperately needed a shower, and Samuel simply pointed him in the right direction. Twenty minutes later, Chris emerged in a white bathrobe emblazoned with the hotel's insignia. Barefoot on the carpeted floor, he sat on a wooden chair, sipping a cold beer from the mini fridge.

Samuel, still in his army shorts and green shirt, had removed his boots and baseball cap. He now wore green slip-ons and sipped his own beer.

"Get some rest," he said, noting the fatigue in Chris's eyes. "You'll need it."

Chris looked around the room approvingly. Two double beds stood under bright mosquito netting. The beddings were a splash of red, yellow, pink, and turquoise. Each bed boasted three plump pillows in blue cases. They looked more than inviting. He didn't even glance at the 50-inch TV in the corner. It was far too late for anything else.

* * * * * * * * * *

Six and a half miles away, I'm struggling to sleep, despite the clock nearing 3:00 a.m.

After Scarlett and I left the mini-theatre, we'd had some light snacks with Alfred. Alex was nowhere in sight. Alfred mentioned he was tying up loose ends and awaiting good news from his team regarding Chris, news that brought a hopeful smile to Alfred's face and a quiet storm of emotions to mine.

Tomorrow, we'd visit Kathleen, Alfred had said. That's What's keeping me awake now, along with the possibility that Alex might return with an update about my brother.

Scarlett, my sweet Scarlett, sleeps peacefully beside me. I envy how easily she disconnects from the whirlwind we've been caught in. For me, it's all still raw.

Kathleen is in a hospice, Alfred told us. Scarlett and I, both healthcare professionals, understand exactly what that means.

Hospice care focuses on providing comfort and dignity to terminally ill patients and supporting their families. The goal is quality of life, not cure—offering physical, emotional, and spiritual care, often from a multidisciplinary team. It can happen at home, in hospitals, or dedicated hospice centers.

I picture Kathleen in bed, tubes, machines, pain. And I wonder if the trauma from her abduction and the years of hiding contributed to her decline. The thought twists something in me.

Scarlett fell asleep quickly, as always. I switched on the computer and began researching breast cancer, something I used to excel at in university. Though I already knew some of the facts, I needed more.

Breast cancer has no single known cause. It emerges from a complex mix of genetic, hormonal, and environmental factors. Age, family history, reproductive history, and lifestyle choices like smoking, drinking, and obesity all play a role.

But Kathleen? From what Alfred said, she didn't fit most of those profiles.

One detail lingered: not breastfeeding, a risk factor. Could that have been it?

As I lie awake, my mind spins, imagining our first meeting, dreading seeing her in such a state, praying that Chris is found. And wondering: *What kind of mental state will he be in?*

* * * * * * * * * *

Meanwhile, more than six thousand miles away in South East London, Marcus sits in his study with four men.

Dressed in a black cardigan, blue jeans, and black sandals, he leans back behind his desk, a cigar clamped in the corner of his mouth. Two silver balls roll in his left hand as he studies the men before him.

Alphonso and Jorum sit next to each other, flanked by two sharply dressed men in grey suits and white shirts, no ties. They resemble businessmen, complete with clear glasses and subtle earpieces that disappear into their collars. They sit in silence, waiting for Marcus to speak.

"I've outlined the key points," Marcus finally says. "Time is of the essence. We need to move within twenty-four hours. The payout will be, massive."

He turns his gaze to the men in suits.

"You know what to do. I'll conclude by wishing you good hunting. I look forward to hearing of your success. Alphonso will drive you to the airport. Everything you need will be waiting with your contact."

With a cursory wave, he dismisses them. The four men rise.

But just as they begin to file out, Marcus stops them.

"Jorum, stay. I have... *special* news for you."

Jorum hesitates. Alphonso shoots him a hard glare. Jorum sits back down.

CHAPTER THIRTY-EIGHT

Samuel is used to getting up early, although this time he is rising earlier than usual. Still, he feels that his body clock has adjusted enough to the time difference, the two-hour gap between here and England, with Mombasa being two hours ahead of GMT, Greenwich Meridian Time. Sometimes, he used to miss this country of his birth and would ponder how every time zone in the entire world was determined from GMT, but had never worried himself enough to delve into it.

He is accustomed to early starts from the days of being married to that bitch Wendy, he recalls as he leaves the shower and gets himself dressed in the same shorts and T-shirt he had only removed earlier. One thing he does not miss about his country of birth is the heat, especially down here on the coast. He had been born in Mombasa and is glad to be back home, albeit under different circumstances. He is pleased that fate had conspired for him to know Marcus and to meet Chris, whom he thought had been dealt a cruel hand by fate—one made even more cruel by Marcus. He is happy to look at Chris sleeping in the next bed as if he didn't have a care in the world.

Samuel was in a dead-end job. He wasn't fooling himself; he knew that he would get very little in the way of benefits, if any, if he stayed until retirement or was made redundant. He was a brilliant accountant, after all, he reminds himself as he thinks about the plans for the day ahead. Being born in Mombasa gave him a slight advantage in that he knew the lay of the land—although advantage over who remained a question in his head.

He sat down on one of the wooden chairs in the room and looked out the window at the brilliant sunshine bathing the place in bright luminescence, listening to the chatter of people going about their business. One thing that had always served Samuel well was a nose for knowing when bullshit was around the corner, and he had smelled it the moment he met Marcus. The more he got to know him, the more he coaxed out of him, without Marcus even realising it. Samuel felt he was in a very good position to strike gold.

He still kept in contact with his family in Mombasa, although some had moved to different parts of the country, some had died, and some he simply had no contact details for.

Marcus was of the disposition that things happened in mysterious ways, but he was a firm believer that everything happened for a reason. He often opined that for every action, there was always an equal and opposite reaction, or as people termed it, karma. His motto had always been: "Do unto others as you would have them do unto you."

He had a careful plan and hoped to execute it perfectly. If it went according to plan, he would never have to bother going back to his corner booth office and auditing meaningless invoices. He looked at a clock on one of the walls, it was just past midday, and as hunger stirred, he began thinking about what they would eat before properly getting accustomed to the place.

Alfred was an early riser. He sometimes stated that sleep was a waste of valuable time. He had a lot to accomplish today; the wheels had already been set in motion, and he was aware that the hardest thing to do would be to take Joe—Joshua—to meet his biological mother in the place he had hoped never to revisit. But fate was beyond even his brilliant mind, the same mind that had built his business empire. He was glad that Alex had done what he had promised and had seen Joe/Joshua safely home.

He often wondered what had happened to James. He never referred to him as Chris, and half of him felt complete now that one of his heirs was safely under his roof. He was a firm believer in God and believed that it was God who had seen them through all that they had endured. He was eternally grateful and had vowed never to question God, never to ask why. Why they had been set up. Why they had to flee their country while Kathleen, his lovely Kathleen, was pregnant with their twins. Why, after settling in a beautiful part of England, they had been abducted and kept hidden from the world for two years.

He had made a promise to his wife that he would never seek revenge or wreak havoc on their enemies.

He thanked God for blessing him with all he had. The balance, he often said to himself, was his wife having breast cancer, and he himself having heart failure. Once again, the thought crossed his mind: what God gives in one hand, He takes away with the other.

But Alfred was happy...as happy as a man losing his beloved wife and dying slowly himself could be. His utmost joy was knowing that everything was in place for

Joe/Joshua to inherit what was rightfully his. From what he had been briefed about him, he knew his son was meticulous, had a kind heart, and was a good academic. He believed that, being young enough, his son would use the vast resources at his disposal to look for and find his brother.

Alfred had also arranged for a DNA test to confirm to Joe/Joshua that they were biologically related.

He was in his plush study, having just finished a conference call with four of his senior vice presidents. They were always happy to hear from the old wise man. Alfred then placed a call to his lawyer, a bright, articulate man in his mid-forties named Amos, and they spoke for the best part of an hour before ending the call.

Alfred lay back in his comfy leather seat, placed his interlocked hands behind his head, surveyed his opulent office-study, and smiled. He closed his eyes and said a small prayer of thanks to God.

I get up just after midday and Scarlett is nowhere to be seen. I guess she hadn't wanted to disturb me when she got up. I reach for the remote control on the bedside cabinet, flick on the huge TV, and tune into a news channel. I like to keep abreast of global events, but nothing interesting is on. I flick through most of the channels and I'm amazed, there are more here than on my Sky box back home. But then again, nothing surprises me anymore on this journey of discovery.

I think about the day ahead. I'm thrilled that I'll be meeting my biological mother, but at the same time, I feel a pang of anger that she's slowly dying. Life can be so cruel; I think to myself. I can't begin to imagine having all these untold riches, being able to buy anything but not being able to save yourself or your wife from the harsh, unforgiving jaws of death. Such is fate, I surmise, as I get out of bed and begin getting ready to face the daunting events awaiting me today.

I wear beige shorts and a white T-shirt after showering. I head downstairs and find Scarlett in the living room, sipping a cold drink and chatting with Allegra and Aurelia. She beams a bright smile when she sees me and beckons me to join them on one of the plush sofas.

"Sleepyhead is finally awake," she says, pulling me close and giving me a peck on the cheek.

Scarlett, whatever she wears, simply stands out. Today, she's in silk leggings (me neither) and a loose blue top. Her hair is held up in a neat bun, and even without makeup, she's just lovely.

I sit next to her and Allegra asks what I'd like to eat. I say I'm not really hungry and would settle for a very cold glass of orange juice. As she leaves the room, Aurelia and Scarlett resume their conversation, about skin tones and makeup. I realise it's not a topic of much interest to yours truly.

There are a couple of magazines on the glass table. I pick one up, it's about investments, shares, and bonds. I realise my life might now have to revolve around things like this. Allegra returns with a tray laden with two jugs, one orange, one green, with two straws and mini umbrellas. I decide not to ask. As we sip our drinks (the green one turns out to be green tea), we make small talk.

I get to know the girls better. They're sisters whom Alfred and Kathleen adopted from a foster home. They say Alfred and Kathleen saved their lives. They're eighteen and sixteen and a half. And for the first time, I notice how beautiful they are (but don't let Scarlett know, a little voice warns in my head). I realise they could be my half-sisters.

* * * * * * * * * *

Six miles away, Chris is now awake and feeling refreshed after a good sleep. He's showered again (he's feeling the heat here), dressed in blue beach shorts, a loose blue T-shirt, brown sandals, and he's applied the sunscreen Uncle Sam bought him. "Not taking any chances," Sam had said.

Wearing black sunglasses, they are now opposite a bazaar, seated at a restaurant enjoying their first meal on the coast. Uncle Sam is explaining the meal options, being from the region originally (Chris knows this well), and claims he's a connoisseur. He urges Chris to try Swahili dishes.

Chris looks at the menu: Biryani, a rice dish with goat, beef, or chicken and spices; Pilau, a fragrant rice dish with meat or vegetables; grilled seafood, including prawns, fish, crab, lobster, and octopus. Also, Viazi Karai (spiced fried potatoes), Mishkaki (grilled meat skewers), and Mhamri (coconut doughnuts).

Uncle Sam orders Samaki wa Kupaka, fish in coconut and chili sauce, plus Mbaazi na Mahamri (pigeon peas with Mahamri), and Viazi Karai. He urges Chris to try the Biryani rice since he knows Chris loves rice.

For drinks, they choose from Bungo juice, freshly squeezed from the local citrus fruit, or smoothies and tropical juices

After eating, they stroll through the town, taking in the sights under the unrelenting sun. Samuel keeps checking his mobile, as though expecting a message. Chris notices.

"Where to now?" he asks as they take a breather at a roadside café, sipping ice-cold mineral water.

Samuel checks his watch, wipes beads of sweat from his brow, and takes a long sip. "It's almost time," he replies. "I'll get the signal soon. Then you'll meet your real father—and your twin brother."

Others might be fazed by something like this. Not Chris. He's composed. What excites him most is meeting his twin. He adjusts his sunglasses, leans back, and watches the beautiful women walking past in beachwear of all sorts.

He feels like he's going to be right at home in this country.

* * * * * * * * * *

Coincidentally, as Chris and Uncle Sam sit enjoying their ice-cold drinks, admiring the local scenery, two mixed-race men are landing at Jomo Kenyatta International Airport in Nairobi on a British Airways flight from Heathrow. They had left not long after departing Marcus's place in southeast London.

They check the signs for the transit exit, they only have a short stopover before their connecting flight to Moi International Airport in Mombasa.

No longer in grey suits, they now wear brown and black cargo pants, brown safari boots, black polo shirts, dark sunglasses, and wide-brimmed Marks & Spencer hats.

They hustle to their next flight and are just settling in as the pilot begins his short announcement, letting the passengers know: the flight will take just one hour.

CHAPTER THIRTY-NINE

It is six o'clock in the evening when Alfred, Scarlett, and I are sat in the most comfortable car I have ever been in. It is a Range Rover Sport with so much room inside, it feels like a stretch limousine. The interior is magnificent. After seeing the car outside the entrance, which was baffling, considering Scarlett and I had roamed the grounds last night and hadn't seen any hint of a car or garage, we got in, and I have to say, this is the kind of vehicle I want to own.

Alfred is sitting in front next to the driver, a man in his early thirties wearing an earpiece. He introduced himself as Martin, bowing as he did so, which I found a bit odd. The car starts rolling down the driveway we saw last night, and I marvel at the luxurious, high-quality interior. Needless to say, there is advanced technology: large touchscreens with haptic feedback on the back of the front seats and meticulous attention to detail throughout. This particular Range Rover Sport SV boasts a cabin finished in leather and Alcantara, carbon-fibre-backed sports seats, soft-close doors, and, wait for it, a fridge in the centre console and "hot stone" massage seats.

Peering between the front seats as the driver brings this magnificent beast to a stop at a gatehouse, I can see a sophisticated infotainment system. I can only imagine the joy of driving something like this. It must contribute to a truly modern and intuitive experience.

The gatehouse is manned by two broad-shouldered, clearly armed men, one on each side. I can't tell exactly what kind of guns they carry, but this time I'm not afraid like I had been at the magistrates'' court. CCTV cameras are everywhere, and the two guards are methodically passing gadgets over the Car's exterior. It's obvious they are seasoned professionals, especially with their boss inside the vehicle.

The wide gates open slowly, revealing another set of tall, imposing gates. These are unmanned and built from what appears to be marine-grade anodised aluminium, a material known for its strength and resistance to rust. More cameras and intercoms flank these gates. As they begin to swing open, a majestic driveway comes into view, lined with the most beautiful flowers I have ever seen. The same lilac, blue, and crimson lights we saw while walking around the mansion the previous night are interspersed along the drive.

At the end of this driveway stands another gate, this one made of reinforced steel and manned by two more armed men. We Aren't held up; the gates are already halfway open as we approach. These two guards are dressed in all black. I don't get a good look at their faces, but I spot a building next to the gate with four massive screens inside. Just before the car turns left onto a new road, I glimpse mine and Scarlett's photos on two of the screens.

What Scarlett and I don't see is a black Land Rover parked near the gate. As our driver pulls away, it follows, carrying three armed men with earpieces and wires disappearing into their collars. Another black Land Rover replaces the first, two armed men now stationed to watch the gate.

The drive isn't long. Scarlett and I watch through the dark-tinted windows. We arrive at the place where I'm to meet my biological mother. I feel apprehensive—there are no words to describe the feeling. The place isn't huge; I'd expected something akin to a general hospital, but I'm glad it's more modest.

After Martin parks the car, we sit in silence. Martin opens Alfred's door, and he steps out to confer with Martin. Scarlett and I follow. The heat hits us instantly. I notice the same black Land Rover parked two cars away; two men now stand beside Alfred, who continues speaking with Martin. They show no weapons, but something tells me they are Alfred's bodyguards.

Alfred finishes speaking and turns to us. "It is time," he says, taking my hands in his. We begin walking toward the main entrance. The grounds are immaculate, with manicured gardens and water features, creating a sense of tranquility and luxury. The entrance features elegant design, high-end materials, and advanced security features. Martin waits for us in a cordoned-off, covered driveway.

The glass doors lead into a spacious lobby with marble floors and custom furnishings. The impression is one of exclusivity and sophisticated care. Signage is understated, not flashy. The two men from the Land Rover enter behind us but say nothing, taking positions inside the entrance.

Alfred leads us further inside, where three women wait. Two are in nurses" uniforms; the third appears to be a doctor. They stand in line as Alfred approaches, Scarlett and I in tow. The lobby is designed to be comforting and informative, reflecting a philosophy of compassionate care. There is natural light, comfortable seating, and access to information via touchscreens and brochure cabinets. A middle-aged couple sits quietly on a plush sofa, holding hands. They seem somber, likely here to visit a loved one.

The reception desk is manned by four staff, three women and one man, all speaking into headsets. The space exudes calmness and excellent organisations, clearly intended to put visitors at ease.

* * * * * * * * * *

Approximately eight miles away, Samuel and Chris are climbing into a blue Nissan Almera. They both sit in the back as Samuel gives the driver directions. Chris remains silent; Uncle Sam has told him this is his moment of truth, a chance to come to terms with his destiny.

The car isn't luxurious, but the air conditioning is a relief from the stifling heat. Chris drinks copious amounts of still mineral water to stay hydrated. Uncle Sam, though less fazed, wipes sweat from his brow with a handkerchief. Chris studies him. Funny how many conversations they've had, yet Chris never truly examined his face. From the right-side seat, he sees a man battling inner demons.

He's never asked Uncle Sam his age, but guesses he must be around sixty. He's clean-shaven, with dark brown eyes and thinning black hair. He wears reading glasses and looks you straight in the eyes during meaningful conversations. Chris turns back to the window. The traffic is heavy.

"We're almost there now, Samuel," the driver says, eyes fixed ahead.

"Thanks, Tony," Samuel replies, lost in thought again.

Tony, or Anthony, is the son of Eliud, a friend Samuel kept in touch with since emigrating from Mombasa. Eliud never moved and hadn't passed away, unlike many others Samuel once knew. Over the years, Samuel had occasionally sent Eliud money. Now, in a twist of fate, Eliud had returned the favour by arranging transport for Samuel.

Though Samuel didn't tell Eliud the full story, Eliud knew of Alfred's reputation, his company had built schools, health centres, and sponsored students abroad. It was also common knowledge that Alfred's wife, Kathleen, was gravely ill. The hospice was reportedly built by Alfred's company to care for terminal patients and was free.

Tony drives them up to a pristine white building surrounded by manicured gardens and water features. Chris notes the elegance and advanced security: CCTV cameras everywhere. He spots luxury cars, notably a Range Rover Sport parked in a cordoned, covered area, a standout vehicle.

His eyes then catch a black Land Rover parked nearby. A man stands beside it, wearing an earpiece, clearly security. Chris is aware of their purpose. Uncle Sam briefed him on Kathleen's condition. Chris had learned more since overhearing Marcus's madness from outside his study. Samuel had hinted that life would never be the same after today. Samuel, too, hoped for a change, though he wasn't doing this for gain. He genuinely wanted Marcus to pay for his sins.

Samuel knew if Marcus found out he helped Chris escape, he'd be hunted. He had no desire to end up in Marcus's crosshairs.

"It's time, Chris," Samuel says, opening his door.

Chris does the same. All six-foot-eight of him steps out into the heat. Samuel gives Tony final instructions. They shake hands, and Tony drives off.

Chris looks at Samuel. Together, they stride forward toward the glass doors and enter a spacious lobby with marble floors and custom furnishings.

CHAPTER FORTY

The two mixed-race men exited the plane at Moi International Airport in Mombasa. After passing through immigration, where the clerk confirmed that Errol and Winsome Jones, brothers visiting on holiday, had all the required documents and stamped their passports, they proceeded to customs, collected their baggage, and entered the arrivals hall. A man awaited them there. He wasn't holding a placard with their names; instead, he scanned his phone, matched their faces to photos, and approached discreetly.

Without breaking stride, he cleared his throat and said quietly, "Follow me, please."

He led them out into the moist evening air and toward a grey, nondescript Toyota Corolla. Slipping behind the wheel, he popped the boot open, fastened his seatbelt, and waited. Errol and Winsome got into the back seat from either side. As soon as they were settled, the driver, who never introduced himself, checked his rear-view mirror, then the side mirror, and pulled smoothly out of the parking lot. There wasn't much traffic leaving the airport. As the car drove into the city, Errol and Winsome each stared out their respective windows, silently taking in their surroundings.

They looked nothing like the brothers described in the immigration records. Errol stood tall at six feet with a lean, muscular frame and not an ounce of fat. Winsome, in contrast, was shorter at five-foot-six, with bulging biceps stretching the fabric of his T-shirt, clearly a man who frequented the gym and probably flipped tractor tires for fun. Errol was clean-shaven, save for a long scar running from his left ear to his jaw, a souvenir from past conflicts. Winsome wore a neatly trimmed beard and moustache.

They were mercenaries, guns for hire, and among the criminal underworld, their reputation was ironclad: they never failed a mission and never left witnesses. As Errol often said, "Dead men tell no tales."

This mission was different. Marcus had briefed them personally, and though they typically chose their contracts, Errol (the unspoken leader of the duo, though Winsome would never admit it) had accepted out of loyalty. Marcus had once helped him financially during a life-threatening crisis, when his mother's life hung in the balance, and Errol hadn't forgotten.

Marcus had only called on them once before, concerning a young man named Chris, who Marcus suspected of stealing drugs. That incident had fizzled out; Marcus had handled it in his own way. Now, here they were again.

Soon, the Corolla pulled into Castle Holiday Apartments. The driver escorted them to a ground-floor unit, tucked out of sight from the main entrance. They wheeled their suitcases inside and looked around. On one of the twin beds sat a locked black case. The driver opened it, glanced at the two men, and said, "I'll be waiting in the car. Don't take long." Then he left.

Errol and Winsome began changing out of their travel clothes. Errol opened the case and was pleased with what he found: two fully automatic firearms, capable of sustained fire with a single pull of the trigger. No instructions were needed. They quickly prepared for the mission.

Forty minutes later, the Corolla rolled away from Castle Holiday Apartments. The men inside bore no resemblance to the ones picked up at the airport. Now they wore black long-sleeved tops, black trousers, steel-toe boots, and black beanies. Each carried a bulging black holdall.

Errol looked at Winsome, fist-bumped him, and grinned. "Clock's on."

* * * * * * * * * *

Six thousand miles away, Jorum lay beaten and bruised on his bed, his head pounding. Alphonso and Marcus had worked him over after driving Errol and Winsome to the airport. Marcus had interrogated him in his study, furious and half-drunk, demanding to know Chris's whereabouts. He accused Jorum of forming a forbidden friendship with Chris, a major offense among Marcus's bodyguards and "nephews."

Jorum had played dumb, claiming ignorance about Chris's escape from the hospital. Marcus had no idea Chris had a hidden phone, or a small safe under his bed. The real truth was, Jorum didn't know where Chris had gone, and even if he had, he wouldn't have told Marcus.

When Alphonso returned, the real beating began. Hands, feet, fists, Marcus was relentless, growing more intoxicated and more violent as the hours passed. Eventually, exhausted, he ordered Alphonso to lock Jorum in his room without food or water. Jorum passed out and only regained consciousness the next day.

His face was swollen, his nose broken, his lips bloodied. Turning in bed was agony. He crawled toward the door, locked. He pressed his ear against it, hoping to hear signs of a guard, but all he could detect was a high-pitched ringing in his ears.

He slumped back onto his bed, trying to find a position that didn't throb with pain. As he shifted, something fell from his pocket. It was his phone. He stared at it in disbelief, the screen cracked but still functioning. Who could he call?

Then he remembered: Samuel. The man who hated Marcus. Samuel had once given him the code to the safe under Chris's bed, where Jorum had retrieved his passport. On his jogging routes, he'd also secretly delivered a manila envelope to Chris. That had been the last time Jorum saw him.

Now, as the pain coursed through his body, Jorum remembered the conversation Marcus had with Errol and Winsome before they departed. He realized he might still do something right, warn Samuel about the plan.

He looked at the phone again. The screen flickered but responded to his touch. With aching fingers, he scrolled to Samuel's number.

He pressed "Dial."

And waited, his breath caught in his throat.

CHAPTER FORTY-ONE

Alfred is very warmly welcomed by the staff here at the hospice, and I can feel the warmth as well. Alfred introduces us and we all shake hands. The doctor asks us to follow her, which we gladly do, as Alfred and the doctor continue to talk. We are led into a very pristine and airy room with a medium-sized table in the middle, flanked by eight comfortable-looking chairs. All the walls are painted white, and the lighting in here is a soft, warm glow of blue and purple. There is a huge TV screen on one end of the wall, with a long white cabinet underneath it, and on top of the cabinet is a phone console. A computer stands solitary in the middle of the table.

The doctor asks us to take seats, and we all sit down, including the two nurses who sit on each side of her. She introduces herself as Doctor Kuzi and lets us know that she is the medical director. She asks if we would like anything to drink, but we all politely decline. She then allows the two nurses to introduce themselves; they state that they are palliative staff nurses, Stacey and Cassandra. They are immaculately turned out in their crisp white uniforms, and there is an overall air of tranquillity about this whole place that I find overwhelming.

Scarlett and I are not holding hands as the doctor starts to speak again, explaining that she is responsible for ensuring that patients receive appropriate care and treatment. This includes reviewing patient care and working with the entire hospice team to develop a comprehensive care plan addressing the patient's medical, emotional, and spiritual needs. I realise that this is directed at me, but I already know all about the different roles played by members of a multidisciplinary team in hospital settings, as does Scarlett. Still, we don't say anything, the last thing I want to show is a lack of respect.

Doctor Kuzi methodically tells us that she leads a team of palliative doctors who specialise in providing comprehensive medical care focused on improving the quality of life for patients with serious, life-limiting illnesses. She leads the medical team to manage symptoms, offer pain relief, and provide holistic support to patients and their families. She goes on to explain that palliative nurses assist patients in maintaining their daily activities, supporting them with personal care, and coordinating other carers if required. By doing so, they enable patients to continue living in their preferred environment for as long as possible.

Alfred doesn't say anything, but after the doctor continues for another few minutes, he says, "Thank you so much, doctor," and stands up, and we all follow his lead. I can tell the occasion is getting to him, but he has already told me that his life is now spent mostly by his wife's bedside—even though she tells him off for "neglecting" himself, urging him to carry on with his life. Not in an angry tone, he had explained, but because she is one of the most selfless people he's ever met. He is glad that she became his wife, his rock, his partner in life.

We follow Doctor Kuzi out of the room and turn left into the brightly lit corridor that we had walked down earlier from the marble lobby. As we walk through more immaculate, brightly lit corridors, we pass different types of staff, and this place feels more like a home than a hospital. I feel calm inside this facility. We slowly walk past individual rooms that appear quite welcoming. The staff are all immaculately turned out in white uniforms, and there is an overall air of tranquillity. Scarlett and I are now holding hands, walking sombrely as we near the location where my biological mother is being nursed during her final days. It feels surreal.

We finally arrive at a medium-sized room, and the doctor allows Alfred to go in first, followed by Scarlett and me. We find ourselves in the cleanest room I've ever entered, and sitting upright on the bed is the most relaxed and calming face I have ever had the chance to look at in my life.

There she is—my biological mother.

Alfred stands beside the bed and gently gives her a hug. As I stand there rooted to the spot, I'm at a loss for words. I can see so much of myself in this face I am looking at. I don't notice her pale face or the blotchy, bluish skin on her hands. She's sitting there, looking at me, a wide smile forming across her lips, and I can tell it's hurting her just to be sitting up.

"Hello, Joshua," are the first words that come out of her mouth.

I gently move forward to the opposite side where Alfred is standing. I look into her brown eyes, exactly like mine, and I cannot help but shed a tear. I reach out and embrace her slowly, careful not to hurt her in any way. For the first time since I got here, I want to say thank you, Dad. I look at

Alfred and silently mouth the words. I feel an uncontrollable urge to just hold this woman in my arms forever. I let go, and we hold hands as she continues to smile at me.

"And this must be the lovely Scarlett," she says as Scarlett stands next to me and leans in for a hug.

"Wow, your father wasn't kidding," she intones in a light-hearted voice. "She is quite attractive, if I must say so myself."

This feels surreal. My father. My mother. Life coming full circle.

"Sit, sit," she says, and we settle into very comfortable seats next to her bed. I sit closest to her, still holding her right hand in my left. I look at this woman and cannot begin to fathom the life she must have had—the struggles she faced, building a company, fleeing the country while pregnant with Chris/James and me, their lives disrupted, abducted—what kind of hell she and Alfred must have endured. It is a true testament to her resolve, as my father has been telling me. Somehow, I feel comfortable calling him that now.

Her hand is cool to the touch, probably due to reduced circulation, but she grips mine tightly, and it feels very safe. I had been warned that her condition would bring increased sleepiness and loss of appetite. Alfred had told me to be prepared for what I would see, but here I am, holding her hand, feeling a gentle calm wash over me. I am not overcome with grief despite knowing I am looking at my birth mother in her failing body, preparing for death.

Doctor Kuzi, standing opposite where Alfred is seated, begins to explain how the cancer has ravaged my mother's body. I glance at my mother, wondering if she wants to hear this now, but she squeezes my hand, looks into my eyes, and says, "It's alright, Joshua. It is my illness, and There's nothing I haven't already heard. Don't be alarmed, she just wants to explain."

As she speaks, I hear a rattling in her voice, fluid in her lungs. I squeeze her hand back and turn my gaze back to the doctor, who has allowed the moment between my mother and me to pass. The doctor speaks in the gentlest voice I've ever heard, and as she continues, Scarlett takes hold of my right hand in both of hers. The doctor is explaining why the skin may appear mottled, with blotchy discolouration, and tells us that my mother is the most resilient woman she's ever encountered in her career.

"Oh, don't be so modest, Doctor Kuzi," says my mother with a short wave of her left hand. "I don't know the woman she's describing," and she chuckles softly, which triggers a coughing fit and more rattling. Doctor Kuzi leans forward and takes her wrist while my mother tightens her grip on my hand.

"It's okay, I'm alright, it will pass," she says after regaining her composure.

I can see why the doctor said she's one of the most resilient women. I see it in her brown, steely eyes. She doesn't want to give up. The cancer may be winning, but she is treating it like just another illness she is determined to overcome.

Doctor Kuzi takes her leave and closes the door. We sit, and my father starts telling a story that makes my mother smile, and it feels like a warm family atmosphere.

* * * * * * * * *

Chris and his uncle Sam had just stepped past the spacious glass doors of the hospice when Chris noticed two security guards outside staring at him in disbelief. They began whispering among themselves. Inside the lobby, two burly men dressed entirely in black were seated, scanning the entrance. Their presence wasn't casual—they looked like they were waiting for someone.

Chris had an instinct for spotting trouble where it shouldn't be. He hadn't survived the streets of his city by being naïve. He'd learned to watch everything—especially for cops. As soon as he laid eyes on the two men in the lobby, his alertness sharpened. He was about to speak to his uncle when Sam's phone rang.

The two men stood up abruptly, but didn't approach. Sam, already on edge, glanced at the caller ID and answered the phone, stepping slightly away from the reception desk to hear more clearly. It was Jorum.

* * * * * * * * *

Six thousand miles away, Jorum was just grateful that the call had gone through despite the cracked screen of his nearly ruined mobile phone. He stood slowly, wincing in pain as he tried to make out Samuel's voice through the faint connection.

"Hello, Samuel, can you hear me?" he half-whispered, half-shouted into the phone.

He tried to keep his voice low. He was fairly sure there was no one guarding the door outside, and anyway—who would Marcus have put there? One of his skinny little "nephews"?

"Hello, Jorum," Sam said from the hospice, turning slightly away from the reception desk, where three women and a man wearing headsets bustled through paperwork and hushed conversations.

Chris stood nearby as his uncle cupped one ear with his hand, straining to catch the conversation. A couple, possibly married, rose from a nearby couch as a receptionist beckoned them forward. Chris noted their faces—drawn, weary. No one looked happy in a place like this.

The two men in black remained rooted where they were. One glanced casually out the glass doors, but the other watched Chris and Samuel closely. Chris's unease deepened. Something was off.

He looked back at Sam, who was now whispering rapidly into the phone, glancing from the men in black to the front desk, his expression turning grim. Whatever he was hearing, it wasn't good.

A few minutes later, Sam disconnected the call and slid the phone back into his pocket. Chris was about to ask what was wrong when Sam leaned in close and said, in a calm, deliberate whisper, "Don't look at those two men. Just follow my lead. We're walking over to that desk. Do not look back."

They moved together, slowly, with practiced calm. The two men didn't move from their spot. One kept watching Chris and Sam, the other glanced again outside.

* * * * * * * * *

Meanwhile, the Toyota Corolla had left Castle Holiday Apartments and was now just five minutes from the hospice.

Errol and Winsome sat in the back, dressed in long white coats draped over their black clothing. Beneath those coats, their boots were laced, their holdalls full. The coats made them look like doctors—or at least like they belonged.

Errol liked this setup. Hospitals made for clean exits. No one expected violence here. No one carried guns. He'd done dozens of jobs, in back alleys and boardrooms and abandoned warehouses, but this—this would be easy.

The driver turned off the main road into a driveway marked with a sign: **KATHLEEN KEYNUDHIA FOUNDATION HOSPICE**.

They entered a polished parking lot filled with expensive cars. The driver pulled into one of two empty spaces near the entrance. He looked into the rearview mirror.

"You remember what to do?" he asked. "Five minutes max. In and out. I'll keep the engine running."

Errol gave a small nod. Winsome, sitting quietly, was studying the building. It was peaceful here. The gardens were manicured, the air smelled faintly of flowers. For a moment, he almost regretted what they were about to do. But a debt was a debt.

Errol, on the other hand, was pumped. Focused. He checked his watch. Everything looked good—minimal foot traffic, no crowds, and only two guards outside, casually chatting. They hadn't even glanced at the Corolla.

Errol and Winsome opened their doors almost in sync and stepped out. They closed the doors quietly, Winsome a second after Errol. Each of them carried two plastic bags—

ordinary, unthreatening. Their faces calm, expressions unreadable.

They began walking toward the hospice entrance, slow and steady.

CHAPTER FORTY-TWO

Samuel approaches the man, who is no longer speaking into his headset and now stands beside a couple engaged in a deep conversation with the woman who had called them over. Samuel cannot make out What's being said.

"And how may I kindly help you, sir?" the man asks politely. From his name tag, Samuel sees he's being addressed by Mr. Kitemu, who wears a broad smile and seems genuinely friendly.

With a slight hesitation, Samuel speaks. "I've received information that those two men standing by the main entrance are here to harm Mrs. Keynudhia." As he says it, he glances over his shoulder and spots the two men still stationed by the door—one now focusing intently on a car that has just pulled up outside, the other watching him and Chris with unsettling attention.

Mr. Kitemu quickly glances beneath the desk—at something Samuel can't see—then looks back at him and Chris. Without a word, he abruptly stands and shouts, "Security!" as his hand slams something underneath the desk.

A shrill alarm erupts, blaring throughout the building.

* * * * * * * * *

At the sound of the sudden, piercing shrill, I let go of my mother's hand and look at my father, who has abruptly stood up. A group of male nurses in blue uniforms rush into the room, surround us, and lock the door behind them.

Scarlett and I get to our feet, confused, wondering what the hell is happening. I assume it must be some kind of drill.

My father looks genuinely alarmed, while my mother remains still on the bed, her breaths coming in short, shallow gasps.

Scarlett looks deeply worried, and from beyond the room I hear loud shouting, doors slamming, and what sounds like glass shattering.

This is madness. This is a hospice, what on earth could be going on?

* * * * * * * * *

Erroll hears the shrill of the alarms first. He quickly drops the two plastic bags he's carrying and whips out his gun, now fitted with a suppressor. In almost the same instant, Winsome does the same, producing a similar weapon with its own silencer. They both discard the white gowns they're wearing and begin moving more swiftly toward the spacious doors, eyes scanning in all directions at once.

From the vantage point of the Range Rover where he's seated, waiting for his entourage to finish their visit, Martin sees it all unfold. He clocks the two figures dressed in black, exits the vehicle, and pulls out his SIG SAUER P226 pistol. He ducks behind the bonnet, aiming his gun at the two men now approaching the glass doors. Martin knows there are two of Alfred's bodyguards inside—and they're among the best Alfred employs.

* * * * * * * * *

The man who had been watching Samuel and Chris suddenly bolts toward them. "RUN, CHRIS!" Samuel shouts, as they both dart into the corridor leading away from the marble reception.

The brightly lit hallway is swarming with people, and Chris, ahead of his uncle Sam, can't see What's happening behind him, but he isn't about to slow down to find out. From the corner of his eye, he'd caught sight of one of the men in black starting to charge toward them.

His brain screams one thing: *I am not going back to Marcus.*

He keeps bumping into people, not daring to look back. He can still hear pounding footsteps and the shouted warning—

"Stop! Stop right now before I shoot!"

As he rounds a corner and slams into a man in a full blue uniform, sending him sprawling, Chris trips over the man's flailing legs and crashes to the pristine floor, rolling as he falls.

And then, the unmistakable crack of a gunshot rings out from the lobby he just fled.

Six more follow in quick succession.

Then two more.

I can't believe what I've just heard, gunshots. All hell seems to be breaking loose. We're in a hospice, for crying out loud!

I look at my father, who is getting help from four male nurses to make my mother more comfortable, and I stand there with Scarlett, not knowing what to do.

This feels eerily like when Francis got shot outside the magistrate's court. Fear begins to creep into my very being. Shootings don't happen in a hospice!

Two of the male nurses open what I had assumed was just a glass wall on the right-hand side of the room, revealing a much larger space—similar to the one we're in, only bigger. My mother is delicately wheeled inside, and one of the nurses urges Scarlett and me to follow. I let Scarlett go in first.

I'm looking at my father, wondering what he must be going through. It must feel like reliving a nightmare for him, I can only imagine. He hasn't let go of my mother's hand and is whispering reassuring words to her while the male nurses go about their work, meticulous and expert in every movement. I can't help but feel that this is something they were prepared for.

The new room my mother has been taken into is spacious, but I can't focus on that right now, not while someone, or maybe more than one person, is firing guns inside this hospice.

To my surprise, and this is something I hadn't noticed before, in all the panic from the alarm and the gunshots, I realise that each of the male nurses is armed. Well, there you are.

It hits me: my father has arranged round-the-clock protection for my mother. And oddly enough, that thought makes me feel a bit safer.

* * * * * * * * * *

Samuel has been shot in the leg and is sprawled on the floor, with one of the men from the lobby straddling him and talking into a mouthpiece.

The other bodyguard has seen the two figures hurrying from a Toyota Corolla, has noticed the discarded plastic bags and coats, but more alarmingly, he has seen the suppressed guns in their hands as they are now separating, trying to take each side of the lobby. He ducks behind the sofa nearest to him as he hears his colleague shouting for the two figures who have run down the corridor leading into the inner sanctum of the hospice to stop, then the unmistakable sound of his colleague's Glock 17 9mm gun letting off a shot.

At the sound of the gunshot from down the corridor, Erroll opens fire, spraying the glass entrance with a fusillade of six bullets, then ducks to the side, away from anyone trying to see him from inside the hospice, but not out of sight of Martin, who, from the Range Rover's side crouching by the bonnet, has got a clear shot at the figure that has just fired at his employer's lobby. And with the aim of the good marksman that he is, he lets loose two quick shots that find their nestling place inside Errol's forehead, and it's goodbye and goodnight Erroll as he flops to the ground, most certainly dead.

Winsome, crouching by the opposite side from where Erroll had been standing, cannot believe what he has just seen. Erroll has been cleanly shot and is gone. With a guttural cry, he stands up and spins around to look for the shooter and eyes the black Range Rover, and he does not realise that it will be the last mistake that he will ever make. Because as soon as Winsome has stood up, letting off his guttural cry, the bodyguard who has ducked behind one of the sofas is presented with the easiest target, and as the figure claps his eyes on the Range Rover and brings his gun to bear, he is hit by three Glock 17 9mm shells that tear through the back of his head, spraying brain matter and all kinds of entrails onto the tarmac where his lifeless body lands—and joins them.

Martin quickly ducks down and takes cover, moving to the rear of the Range Rover, using it as cover and waiting to hear if there will be any more gunfire.

The second bodyguard cautiously keeps his gun trained on the Toyota Corolla that is still idling in the car park. He speaks into his mouthpiece, and Martin responds, as well as the first bodyguard, who, amidst a barrage of protests from the man that he has apparently apprehended, shouting all kinds of lawsuits that he is going to file, coming through the earpiece, states that there appears to be one occupant in the driver's seat of the Toyota Corolla.

The second bodyguard can clearly see the driver in the driver's seat, and he can see Martin emerging from behind a row of parked cars and start zigzagging his way towards the back of the Toyota. The bodyguard steps through the shattered glass entrance and, step by step, gun raised and pointed at the Toyota's windscreen, he approaches cautiously, as Martin does the same from the rear. The driver, who has seen everything that has happened before his very eyes, has not been able to move a muscle and is frozen in fear as the second bodyguard stands in front of the car, gun pointing directly at him, and he slowly raises his hands up as far as the small enclosure of the Toyota will let him, whilst at the same time, acting on a signal from the bodyguard, Martin yanks the driver's door open, and the driver is now faced with two guns, a Glock 17 9mm and a Sig Sauer P226 pistol.

"Help," he manages to say in a croaking voice.

Martin methodically asks him to carefully, very carefully, exit the vehicle, as the second bodyguard keeps his Glock trained on him, and he is finally spread-eagled, face-first on the ground. The second bodyguard does a thorough check of the car before joining Martin in order to secure the driver. The driver's hands are zip-tied behind his back, and the second bodyguard leaves Martin with the driver and starts patrolling the area, gun trained in front of him, looking for any signs of movement or anything suspicious. There is not a soul in sight. Anyone who had been at the car park has either gone into their cars, and the bodyguard, who had been looking outside for the duration that they had been stood inside the lobby, recalls that there were roughly about four or five elderly couples in the parking lot. No car has driven off, and no car has entered the parking lot. He continues scanning the area, moving from car to car, and once he is satisfied that there is no other imminent threat, he speaks into his mouthpiece.

"Clear," he says, and moves towards Martin, where the driver is now whimpering and asking for his life to be spared

* * * * * * * * *

Chris has now been surrounded by two male nurses and he has got his hands in zip ties behind his back and has been marched into a back office, which appears to be some holding area. He is not saying a word and is keeping his head down and has not taken his dark sunglasses off. He has not been manhandled, and he can hear Uncle Sam shouting blue murder and threatening all kinds of lawsuits. The room that he has been brought into has got two rows of benches on opposite sides, and in the middle is a wooden table flanked by ten chairs in total. There is a computer desk in one corner of the room with a multitude of workstations on it, as well as a telephone console. The two men, dressed in blue uniforms and clearly armed, who are now standing guard over Chris, are not saying anything, and Chris is keeping his head bowed and wishing that he had not come here. Uncle Sam has clearly been shot, he is now a prisoner of goodness knows who, and he can only contemplate what is going to happen to him from here going forwards.

He shuts his eyes tight and wills himself to be anywhere else but here. He has come too far from the life in the house with Marcus, and everything that he hated about that place comes flooding back to him.

CHAPTER FORTY-THREE

As one of the nurses administers medication to my mother, I realize the room also contains a communications hub, and it dawns on Scarlett and me that this is some kind of escape room.

I discover this as I walk over to speak with my father, who has just gotten off the phone.

He tells me that, so far, there have been three intruders outside, two shot by Martin and Sled, one of his bodyguards, and the third detained inside a car.

He adds that two other unarmed intruders were also apprehended, one shot and wounded by Tommo, his other bodyguard, and a young man was captured unharmed.

He tells me the injured man is being treated under armed guard, and the young man is being held a few offices away. He asks if I'd like to accompany him to speak with the captive, though Alfred suspects they were after him.

As we exit the room and re-enter the corridor, normalcy seems to have returned to the hospice. I can sense these are people accustomed to the extraordinary. After all, caring for people at the end of their lives must be incredibly tough, I think to myself.

We leave Scarlett sitting next to my now-sleeping mother, as she wished. Three armed nurses escort us to the room where the young man is being held—I want to hear what he has to say.

* * * * * * * * * *

Chris is feeling really tired and decides that whatever happens from now on, he would rather die fighting rather than be taken back to that brute. He wonders what will happen to his uncle Sam, he is probably going to get something really bad done to him. Probably even killed, he thinks. He can hear voices coming from outside the room that he is in, and he braces himself, waiting for the worst.

* * * * * * * * * *

The lead male nurse opens a door and Alfred and I file in, and as we do so, Alfred stops mid-stride and freezes in position. I look around him to see what has made him stop, and I freeze on the spot. The two male nurses holding the young man exchange looks, glance at him, then at me, then back at him, and then at me again.

I realise that I am looking at, for the first time, my brother, my twin brother, Chris.

The room goes deadly silent. Alfred and I on one side; Chris, sitting on a bench with his hands behind his back, on the other, flanked by two male nurses.

Without warning, I see Alfred's legs give way and he topples forward. One of the nurses by his side manages to catch him, but not before he hits the edge of the table in the middle with his head, and blood starts coming from his forehead. Another nurse helps to lower Alfred's body to the ground, and it's obvious he's out cold.

I shift my gaze back to Chris, who is looking at me in awe. We're just there — me standing, staring at him; him seated on the bench, staring back at me with his hands behind his back. It's like looking into a mirror.

I suddenly rush forward and give him a huge bear hug, then realise he can't move his arms. I move to the side and see that his hands are tied with zip ties. I tell the nurses — anyone — to quickly remove them, and one of them does so. Chris stands up, shaking his hands loose as if trying to get the circulation back, all the while sizing me up. I'm looking at a complete carbon copy of yours truly, and I cannot come to terms with it. We don't say anything — just looking at each other is enough.

"You must be Joe," Chris breaks the silence as he gingerly looks behind him and sits back down on the bench, still massaging his left wrist.

My goodness, it is actually like looking into a mirror.

"Yeah, I mean, yes. Yes, I'm Joe," I manage to say.

There's no point in confirming he is Chris. His face tells me everything there is to know.

Still massaging his left wrist, he goes on, "And that must be Alfred," gesturing toward Alfred, who has now been placed on a comfortable, plush sofa and is gently coming to.

His head wound has been bandaged. It appears to be a minor cut sustained when he fainted and hit the edge of the table. He still looks shaken and groggy, and as he continues to be looked after by his team, I sit next to Chris.

"Yes," I reply. "That is indeed Alfred."

"And where is his wife, Kathleen?" asks Chris. It seems he wants to know everything right now, and I am just speechless. I don't know what to think. This is Chris, sitting next to me and talking to me. This is James, my twin brother, older than me by five minutes.

Unbelievable, that we have grown up in the same country and were never aware of each other. Looking at him, I feel sorry for the kind of upbringing he must have had. To me, he doesn't look like he's suffering from a mental health disorder, but I'm basing that on feelings. I've finally met someone who, until a few days ago, I'd never even thought about.

"She's here," I say. "Well… not here in this room," I add, suddenly feeling like a child talking to a grown-up after being caught doing something they shouldn't have.

Chris glances around, then looks at Alfred, who appears to be regaining his composure. "Obviously, Kathleen isn't in this room," he says. "But I assume you mean she's in this hospice, right?" He turns and looks at me.

Same colour eyes. Same shaped eyebrows. Jawline. Hair. This is amazing. We appear to be exactly the same height, though not the same build. He is more muscular than yours truly, and I can tell he's well-built and toned. I've seen the baby pictures Alfred showed me of us, but this? This is unreal.

Chris doesn't seem fazed by What's happening. In fact, I sense relief all over him. I'm eager for us to catch up, but There's so much he needs to know. It's going to be an interesting story to tell.

Doctor Kuzi personally escorts us from the room where Chris had been held. Alfred wants to walk unaided, but Doctor Kuzi won't allow it and insists he be ferried in a wheelchair — much to Alfred's consternation and chagrin. Doctor Kuzi reports that my mother is resting and can't stop saying how pleased he is to meet Chris and me. We're told Kathleen is asleep, the events of the last hour or so have taken a toll on her, and that we can see her when she wakes.

It's been really crazy, and funny, introducing Chris to Scarlett. As soon as we leave the room where Alfred hit his head, we're escorted to a small meeting room where hot food and drinks await. Scarlett keeps looking at me, then at Chris, then back at me, as we sit side by side across from her and Alfred, tucking into delicious food, and I can tell she finds this all quite amusing. Chris has commented on how beautiful she is and told me I'm a very lucky man.

Chris comes across as quick-witted and appears comfortable talking about a wide range of subjects. Once Alfred regains his composure, he asks for the wheelchair to be taken away, gives Chris a massive bear hug, and welcomes his other son home. Again, Chris doesn't seem fazed at all, he's taking it all in stride. Alfred takes both of us by the hand, looks long into our eyes, and sheds a few tears. I shed a tear too, but Chris appears more composed and brings us all together in a giant group hug.

Before we sit down to eat, Alfred is told that Samuel is not badly wounded, and he asks for him to be brought in. We all look toward the door as a male nurse wheels in a man who appears to be in his late fifties, with specks of grey hair, reading glasses, grey khaki shorts, black sandals, and a hospital shirt. He's clean-shaven. The nurse props him beside Chris, and Samuel bows in appreciation as the nurse leaves and shuts the door.

Chris has briefly updated us on the role Samuel played in helping him get here, and it seems like tonight is going to be a long one. I joke with Chris, a night of storytelling: the past, the present, and hopefully, the future. I'm so glad Chris made it here, all thanks to this man called Samuel. I can already sense a bond forming between Alfred and him, which I think is a good thing, especially since Samuel mentioned he's an accountant and was born in Mombasa. He says he has so much to tell Alfred, especially about the betrayal by his half-brother Marcus, but Alfred just smiles and nods. He is at peace; his two sons are finally where they belong.

After about an hour of Chris, Alfred, and I catching up on our lives, we are informed that our mother is ready to see us now. Alfred had gone ahead to break the news to her, he didn't want her to have a heart attack at the excellent news.

We enter the room, Chris and I first, followed by Scarlett. Our mother is lying on the bed, propped up by pillows on either side, and as soon as she sees us, tears begin streaming down her face. She reaches out her arms, beckoning us to her. Chris and I both go to her and embrace her warmly, the three of us.

Chris sheds a few tears as our mother says,

"Hello James. Meet your brother Joshua.

Welcome home, my sons, my beautiful, handsome sons."

CHAPTER FORTY-FOUR

Chris sits next to me, and Father sits with Scarlett and Samuel, who, Father has said, will now be treated as part of the extended family after what he did in getting Chris to his birth parents. It all feels very natural, almost surreal in its normalcy. We've had more than enough to eat and drink, and despite the pain our mother is enduring, everyone appears calm and grounded in this moment.

We talk about everything and nothing. Mother can't take her eyes off Chris and me, and I know it's strange for her to see us as James and Joshua. For the first time, I realise how this room has been designed like a home-away-from-home, adapted to give her the warmth and familiarity of her own house. It doesn't feel like a hospice at all. Every aspect of her care has been considered with precision and love.

Father had told us earlier that she doesn't like being fussed over, and I feel a pang of guilt, guilt that she had been robbed of watching her sons grow up. I feel deeply for Chris, especially after hearing fragments of the life he endured with Marcus. I see something simmering in Father—a silent rage, perhaps—but he tempers it with grace.

Looking at us both, Father says, "Revenge is for the weak. Ugly people fall by themselves eventually." Samuel nods in agreement, saying he believes in karma—what goes around comes right back around. He recounts a story about his ex-wife, Wendy, and the more he tells, the more comical it becomes. At one point, Mother bursts out laughing, especially when he mentions calling the police to report her as a missing person. Her laughter is a small miracle.

Scarlett beams, her smile radiant, clearly happy for me, and it shows. Mother drifts off to sleep while we're still gathered around her. The nurses move in to tend to her with quiet dignity, giving her medication and ensuring she's comfortable despite the cancer ravaging her body. None of us feel like leaving, least of all Chris and me.

Samuel, now treated for the leg wound Tommo gave him, is resting in the adjoining room. He said he wouldn't file any lawsuit, grateful that the shot wasn't fatal. He understands now: Tommo and the rest are trained to eliminate threats. The only reason he wasn't killed is that he looked harmless in his beach shorts, with no visible weapon.

Samuel then explained what had happened at reception. The phone call he had received had come from Jorum, one of Marcus's bodyguards, who had warned him that Marcus was now hiring hitmen to track down and kill Chris. Jorum didn't know Chris was in Mombasa with Samuel. When Samuel assured him Chris had escaped, Jorum warned him not to go anywhere near the hospice. Marcus had sent two assassins to kill Kathleen and anyone else in the way.

That was when Samuel had rushed to warn the receptionist. When the alarm was triggered and chaos erupted, it had all stemmed from that warning. Father thanked Samuel again for bringing Chris to him, telling him how hard he'd tried to find his son. He reassured Samuel that he had acted in good faith and even taken a bullet in the process. At that, we all laughed, lightening the mood again.

Still, in the back of my mind, There's one unanswered question: Why would Marcus want to kill our mother when she has only a short time left? It's terrifying to think he even knew where she was.

Sitting on the plush blue velvet sofas (I've learned blue is Mother's favorite color), Scarlett lays her head on my lap, wrapped in a warm golden fleece, sipping pineapple juice through a straw. Chris sits curled up with a mug of cocoa. Father relaxes on a navy-blue chaise lounge with a glass of still water. Samuel sleeps nearby. It all feels like a scene from a life we were meant to have.

Clearing my throat, I ask the question That's been haunting me. "Why would Marcus want to kill our mother if she's already dying?"

Father exhales, reflects, and begins:

"Marcus has had it in for me ever since I became successful. Kathleen warned me to keep him on a tight leash. She never trusted him. He felt entitled, even though Kathleen and I built the company from nothing, he always wanted more. He was unscrupulous then, and he still is."

He pauses, looking at Chris. "I never knew my own father. My mother did the best she could. I filled the void by working hard. Being an only child wasn't hard, but times were."

Another pause. "I do believe in fate. Not coincidences. Fate. Joshua," he says, turning to me, "you were lucky. You were raised by a loving family, not your race, no, but a good family. And Chris... it's time to right that wrong."

Then, softly, "James, you were born five minutes before Joshua. But to me, you're both my sons. No difference. I've made preparations already, but tonight isn't about business. Tonight, we're a family. Finally, And I thank God for Samuel. If you want, we can take a DNA test, just to be sure."

There's a beat of silence. Then he continues, "Sometimes, I think all the angels Aren't in heaven, they walk among us. That's why I believe in fate. If something's meant to happen, it will. My faith has seen me through dark times, but faith needs work too," he chuckles, and we all laugh with him.

"People fall. People break. People fail. But then, people rise. People heal. People overcome. That's what I want to pass on to you. If you have to creep to do it, lie to conceal it, or erase it to hide it, then you shouldn't be doing it."

He stands, walks slowly around the room, and stops beside Kathleen. We can hear him whispering softly to her.

The digital clock behind Chris reads nearly 1:00 a.m.

Scarlett shifts, placing her glass on the table. Chris puts his cocoa mug aside. I stroke Scarlett's hair gently. Everything is calm now, peaceful. And still, we know: outside this room, in other rooms, others are facing their final moments. just like our mother. It's a sobering thought.

"Be courageous, my dear. And astute enough. Sometimes, it's enough to wait for what you deserve," Father whispers, and we hear him clearly this time.

Chris and I lock eyes. No words are needed.

I realise how easy I had it compared to my brother. While I was raised in a loving home, he was passed from foster family to foster family, never truly wanted. I thought I stood out growing up in a white family, but now I know how fortunate I truly was. I was told my parents had died in a car crash, no photos available. I stopped asking. I had grown into my new life, but I never stopped wondering.

And now... here we are.

Father returns to his seat, his shoulders heavy with a life's worth of struggle and resolve. He picks up the half-full glass of water.

"I am the happiest man in the world right now," he says.

He lifts the glass. "Would you say this is half full, or half empty?"

"Half full," Chris replies, without missing a beat.

Father smiles. "Well said. A glass half full reflects hope. Half empty? Cynicism."

Scarlett, always quick, sits up and raises her hand like she's in a lecture hall. Father grins and gestures for her to speak.

"If you surround yourself with positive people who believe in the good, you'll start to see the glass as half full too," she says.

Laughter. Silence. Peace.

And then Father quietly says it's time for bed. He'll stay here to finish some work. We've already been shown the sleeping quarters. Everything has been thought of, for her, for us.It's not just a hospice. It's home.

CHAPTER FORTY-FIVE

The night passes smoothly, and by ten o'clock in the morning, we are all awake. Everyone is fresh and ready for the day, gathered around mother's bedside. I'm surprised to see Alex, my friend the private investigator, already there, along with a few unfamiliar faces. Alex, beaming with his ever-present smile, introduces Maxine, a stunning mixed-race woman around his age, as his beloved wife.

Mother is awake, engaged in quiet conversation with father. Scarlett is chatting with Chris, while Alex introduces me to Jasmine, his twenty-year-old daughter, who is just as beautiful as her mother. Samuel is seated on one of the sofas we used last night, his bandaged leg resting on a stool. He's cradling a hot drink, lost in thought. After meeting him yesterday, I would say he seems a good man, and I like to think I'm a good judge of character.

Soon, the nurses politely usher us away, saying they need to take mother for a procedure and she'll be back in under an hour. Father suggests we move to another room down the corridor, and we all settle around a huge maple table in what is clearly a meeting room. The ensemble now includes Father, Chris, Scarlett, who seems to be hitting it off with Jasmine, Samuel, Maxine, Alex, and yours truly.

While we wait for mother's return, a hearty breakfast is served. Afterward, Father announces we'll be heading back to his house (though calling it a "house" feels like a gross understatement), where we'll address the matters of the day. He shares that the driver of the Toyota has confessed to the police, revealing he had received instructions from Marcus.

Apparently, the driver had worked for the company during Marcus's transfer to Changamwe years ago, and they had become close. The driver had also disclosed the existence of a rented room at Castle Holiday Apartments, which the police have since raided, collecting passports and outbound air tickets as evidence. The bodies of Erroll and Winsome have been taken to the morgue, and, as far as Father is concerned, the police are handling it from here.

I have never felt happier in my life. The past few days have been an emotional rollercoaster, reuniting with Chris, seeing Mother again, nothing could top this.

We're ferried back to Father's mansion in a three-car convoy: Father, Scarlett, and I ride with Martin in a luxurious Range Rover; Alex, Maxine, and Jasmine travel in a sleek black BMW X5; Chris and Samuel are driven in a Land Rover Discovery. An armed escort leads and follows us. After spending a few more moments with mother, just Father, Chris, and me, we leave her to rest, knowing the recent excitement must have taken a toll on her.

The drive feels like an official motorcade. As we turn left to exit the hospice, I glance through the tinted window and notice a sign I somehow missed before: **KATHLEEN KEYNUDHIA FOUNDATION HOSPICE**. I don't know it yet, but I have just seen my mother alive for the last time.

We pass through the gates, but the armed escort vehicles do not follow. Martin parks at the grand entrance, as do the other two drivers. I've never seen the other drivers before. As we step out, I notice two men tending to the lush lawn, and sprinklers cast a gentle mist over the grass. Chris doesn't seem too fazed; we all head inside, where we're greeted by a polite, middle-aged woman I've not met. Father introduces her as Brenda, the chef. Allegra and Aurelia are there too, and they're introduced to Chris—I notice a sparkle in his eyes.

We gather in the same elegant living room Scarlett and I had seen before. Drinks are served by yet another unfamiliar but polite woman named Sheila, part of Father's housekeeping team. The house is bustling with people, but after what we've just experienced at the hospice, the warmth is welcome. Still, a part of me feels guilty about leaving Mother there, though I know she's in the best hands as she approaches the inevitable.

This feels like a warm, intimate gathering. Scarlett sits beside me, and I take her hand as I glance around. Chris is deep in conversation with Samuel, whose foot is now resting on a pillow. Alex is chatting with Maxine, and Jasmine sits between Allegra and Aurelia—they're laughing about something, clearly reconnecting from the time Alex's family had stayed here while Father helped him with a case. Father sits alone, contemplative but with the unmistakable look of a content man. I'm so happy for him.

After a couple of hours of rest, Sheila announces that dinner is ready, and we move to the dining room where a feast awaits.

Father excuses himself for an important matter that will take only a few minutes. The rest of us dive into the meal, it's exquisite. I'm quickly discovering that Alex is a riot—his jokes keep the laughter flowing. Jasmine shares that she's in her final year at King's College studying psychology and psychiatry, which impresses both Scarlett and me. Maxine works at a law firm as the personal assistant to the managing director. Chris listens intently, his curiosity insatiable. When he starts talking about electrical engineering, no one can challenge him, he's clearly an expert, and I'm in awe, knowing the kind of life he's lived. I'm proud to call him my brother and feel a lump in my throat.

Samuel entertains everyone with stories of his marriage, including a few drunken nights spent locked out and in the shed, which he assures us are relics of a past life, the drinking, not the memories, he's quick to clarify.

The day unfolds slowly. Father is visited by various associates in his office. Chris and I attend several meetings, introduced to managers, accountants, and high-level staff. Two elegantly dressed secretaries diligently take notes. These meetings give Chris and me a window into Father's business. I'm impressed. Everyone we meet is kind and welcoming, aware that we're the new co-owners, with Father remaining in an advisory role. They're aware of his health and ask kindly after Kathleen.

That evening, Father hosts a formal dinner to welcome Chris and me. The dining room is grand, with about thirty guests seated at a massive table. Chris and I sit on either side of Father. Everyone is dressed impeccably, men in suits, women in gowns. The seating is clearly curated, with alternating genders. It's the first time Chris and I have worn tuxedos, and we've had a laugh about it.

The table is set with a crisp white tablecloth, gleaming flatware and glassware, and a bouquet centerpiece that enhances the ambiance. As I take it all in, I feel a pang knowing Mother isn't here. I say a silent prayer for her.

Ten uniformed servers, including Brenda, Sheila, and members of the kitchen staff—stand around the table as Father gives thanks: for the food, for family, and for Kathleen. He then gives a heartfelt speech welcoming his sons home. Applause follows. He has always had the power to command a room.

Scarlett sits to my left, with Allegra beside her. Aurelia is next to Chris, along with Alex, Maxine, and Jasmine. The rest of the guests are Father's trusted business associates— the lifeblood of his empire. The room radiates warmth and goodwill.

The meal is served in multiple courses, each accompanied by the appropriate tableware and drink. Conversation flows effortlessly, and the servers tend to us with precision and grace. Afterward, drinks are poured, and the selection is vast. I spot Alex savoring a Macallan, clearly in his element.

Guests begin mingling in the living rooms, where soft music floats from hidden speakers. Chris and I step outside, each with a cold beer. As we walk, we reflect on everything that has transpired. Chris shares that he went to my flat after overhearing my address outside Marcus's office. He laughs, saying he'd wanted to see if what he'd heard was true. He recalls giving money to two women to lie about his visit, just in case Marcus questioned them. He acted on instinct. I laugh and tell him That's when I began suspecting Alex's claims might be true, though the women's story raised doubts.

We sit on a bench overlooking the ocean. A warm breeze brushes past, and stars scatter the night sky. The music drifts outside.

"I'm not bothered about taking a DNA test," Chris says, looking at me. "Honestly, There's no need. Anyone can see we're twins, we both look like Mother and Father in our own way."

I nod. I've felt the same way for a while now. I tell him so, and we decide to share this with Father.

"Hey, let's check out the private beach," I say.

Chris glances back toward the house and grins. "How about we get the girls out here? You know, the more the merrier." I see the twinkle in his eyes.

We don't need to go back inside. Just then, Scarlett walks out, hand in hand with Jasmine, followed closely by Allegra and Aurelia. All four carry cocktail glasses, laughing and smiling.

"There you are!" Scarlett exclaims as she approaches. "Fancy you two gorgeous specimens sneaking off without a word," she teases. I can tell she's a little tipsy. My Scarlett. My dream girl. She's wearing the most stunning dress I've ever seen, hugging her curves just right. I pull her close by the waist. She kisses me softly, and I breathe in the sweetness of her perfume.

In that moment, I am in heaven.

CHAPTER FORTY-SIX

"You know they have prepared all kinds of meat and fish over there," points out Aurelia with her cocktail glass, starting to walk towards the private beach, followed by Allegra. The sisters are wearing matching red gowns and they both look like princesses. Everyone is dressed to the nines, and everyone looks so beautiful tonight, I just want to stay here and never move.

Jasmine, taking a sip from her glass in a straw that she is holding, tells Chris, "You know I am going to have a hard time distinguishing who is who amongst you two," and she giggles, then takes Chris's arm and starts following the sisters towards the private beach, giggling as she does so. Her turquoise figure-hugging dress is setting her out like a goddess, and there is beauty everywhere tonight.

"Oh, That's easy," Chris replies with a broad smile. "I am the eldest one," and he links his arm with hers and beckons for Scarlett and I to join them.

We get to the private beach and sure enough, there are two men, the groundskeepers that we had seen during the day, and they appear busy at the beach grill and bar. There is the sweet, succulent aroma of roast meat in the air and smoke can be seen rising from the barbeques that the men are working on. It feels like we are at an out – door market surrounded by the smell of cooking and aromatic spices.

There are very comfortable seating arrangements, it's akin to having an outdoor restaurant. We can see an array of roast dishes; *nyama choma*, fish, chicken drumsticks and other types of seafood. There's that *kachumbari* that I have come to love so much and there is a table loaded with all kinds of beverages. There is an entertainment system ensconced on the left away from the waters lapping up from the ocean, and Allegra ambles over to it, looks at us and shouts, "Music!!" and booming music emanates from powerful speakers and it feels like a proper party atmosphere. There are about ten tables with four plush seats per table, the floor is made of wooden floorboards and beyond that is gorgeous white sand which leads out to meet the blue waters of the Indian Ocean. Oh, what a night, I am thinking as Chris whips off his bowtie, takes off his tuxedo and grabs another cold beer. He seems so happy and I am genuinely happy for him.

The two men cannot help but laugh at the antics that these six youngsters are carrying on with, they join in with conversation especially with the two sisters and it all makes for a very jovial and entertaining atmosphere.

Soon we are joined by some of the guests who come in by twos and threes. Alex comes holding hands with Maxine and father comes an hour later. He is glad that everyone is having a good time, especially as he looks over at where the six of us have joined two tables and are all sat talking animatedly and laughing, and he feels pride and joy welling up inside him and he says a silent thank you to The Almighty. Everyone seems to be in a party atmosphere, there is lots to eat and drink, the music is playing, the breeze is blowing, there is lovely sounds being made by the waves from the ocean and it seems and feels like a tropical paradise. Deep down we know that there is nothing that can be done to save mother from the awful disease that has ravaged her body and it feels bitter sweet, reuniting only knowing that we would say goodbye soon.

The night carries on until everyone starts peeling away slowly, some guests getting picked up by their drivers and other guests heading to guest quarters that I have not even seen. The servers all help with the clean-up and we head indoors, satisfied, tired but happy. I am just amazed by father's energy. He doesn't seem to get tired and I can tell that it hurts badly, but then again, I remember what he had said, that he would never question his God. He had said that everything happens for a reason, not believing in coincidences and that what God takes away with one hand, he gives with the other. Beneath all the joy that he is feeling, especially after Chris had turned up, must be a mountain of hopelessness that there is nothing that he can do to save his wife, I know. We retire to bed, everyone is shown their sleeping quarters and I stand outside our balcony and stare out to sea, looking at the waves crushing on to the shore and remember something that I had once read somewhere that you cannot swim for new horizons until you have courage to lose sight of the shore.

In the morning, there are not many of us gathered for breakfast, just Chris, father, Scarlett and I, which seems apt for some reason. We have planned to go and spend the day with mother; father is confident that everything that he needed done in the interim has been accomplished. We can hear noises from the kitchen and know that Brenda and her team are busy at work preparing the delicious meals that they are so good at. Father lets us know that his cardiologist has told him that there has been no improvement in his heart condition and that he is to continue with his current course of treatment. He shrugs as he says this, trying to make light of the situation but we know that he is not feeling well although he is trying valiantly to hide it from us. I know that with all that has happened, it's like father's ailment has been put on a back burner and I feel that it should not be forgotten. Father wants to tell us something, he says, something that he feels we as a family including Scarlett should be aware of, as he states that there are no secrets in his family. He states that Chris had told him about Jorum and that he would like to help Jorum, and Chris would love for Jorum to be away from Marcus's clutches.

He explains that Chris has told him that Jorum does have a valid passport and Chris knows that Jorum would love the chance to get away from Marcus. Chris had been heartbroken after his uncle Sam had told him about the beating that Jorum had gotten from Marcus and Alphonso and really wanted to help him. Father says that Samuel had gotten in touch with Jorum that morning on his mobile phone and had instructed him that if he got the chance to leave, even if it was to go out with some of Marcus's "nephews" to deal drugs, he should try to get away and Samuel had given him the name of one of his friends who Marcus had no idea about. The friend would then be able to buy the necessary travel ticket for Jorum and then he would be able to flee the country and join him in Mombasa. Samuel has reported to father just an hour ago that Jorum had been very keen on the idea and that he would be in touch in a short while.

Chris seemed really happy at the idea of Jorum getting away from that brute.

"What's going to happen to that mad man?" he asks father as he puts his mug of coffee on the table and reaches for a piece of the delicious toast that we have just had some of, spreads honey on it and takes a small bite.

Father looks at him thoughtfully and places his fingers around the mug of green tea that is in front of him.

"Son, I don't believe in revenge. Fate will deal with my half – brother, I don't have to do anything. You cannot mess with other people your whole life and go to your grave a happy man. The world always finds a way to catch you up. Everyone gets their comeuppance in the end my son."

I am learning a lot from father and I am glad that Chris and Scarlett are here with me.

"There is something else," father says as he clears his throat. "Joshua wants to call his parents in England and appraise them of what has been happening and he has got my full blessing. I am so pleased for them that you turned out the way that you did, and I am not saying this to heap praise on you because James is right here, but to acknowledge a fact" and with that he bows his head.

Chris gets up and walks over and gives him a huge hug. I follow suit and the three of us are there; Chris and I hugging father as he remains seated with his arms around both of our waists. We stay like this for a few moments and the embrace is broken by Sheila, the head housekeeper, as she clears her throat and we turn around and look at her, standing by the entrance to the dining room.

"You have a phone call from the hospice," she says, addressing father who quickly stands up and tells us to finish our breakfast, he will be back in a moment. Sheila then exits as Chris and I resume our seats and Scarlett has a curious look in her eyes. She takes my hand and grasps it tightly and looks deeply into my eyes.

"That sounds ominous" says Chris in a sombre voice as he takes a sip of his now tepid coffee.

All kinds of thoughts start flushing through my mind. Why would the hospice be calling, they are aware that we are going over to spend today with mother? I start to get thoughts that I don't want to in my head and suddenly father returns and states that we have to go to the hospice now, there is no time to explain.

Twenty minutes later we are in the BMW X – 5 being driven at speed to the hospice, Chris, Scarlett and I at the back and father in front with Martin. There is a Land Rover Discovery behind us, we are not focused on anything else but getting to the hospice. Father has informed us hastily that the team at the hospice has been concerned at the sudden turn in Kathleen's health and were worried that she was slipping away. It was expected, but father had instructed them that if that ever happened, he was to be notified right away. Father is out of the vehicle before it has even come to a complete stop, followed rapidly by Chris and I wait for Scarlett to exit the car and we take off after them. There are a few people in the marble reception but we run straight past, there have been people waiting for father but they are being left in his wake as he makes his way to his wife's room at full pelt. Chris has already overtaken him and he is the first one into the room, the doors are open and father runs in after Chris just as I arrive with Scarlett hot on my heels. Doctor

Kuzi is by mother's bedside, by her head; and there are two other doctors present plus two male nurses. Father stops by the other side of doctor Kuzi and takes hold of mother's hand, who appears as if she is sleeping peacefully; she must be, she's got a smile on her face. Chris is stood next to father with his left hand over his shoulder and his right on father's hands which have got hold of mother's right hand. Father is whispering out mother's name over and over, squeezing her hand gently as Chris continues to hold his hands.

I stand at the end of the bed then move over to where doctor Kuzi is, gently shove her aside and kneel on the floor so that my eyes are almost level with mother's head. I take her left hand which feels cool to the touch, look at her face and just stare at her calmness and the smile that is on her face. Scarlett stands behind me and places her hands on my shoulders, the room is silent and no one says anything, even father has now stopped whispering. I look at mother's face which appears relaxed with her mouth slightly open and I notice that her eyelids are partially open as well.

The other two doctors make their excuses and leave with the two male nurses. Doctor Kuzi walks over to where father and Chris are standing, lays her left hand on father's back.

"Sorry Alfred," she says in a low voice. She must have felt at peace enough to let go and at least now she is pain – free" before gently leaving the room, and we are left there looking at mother. It's like we are willing her to open her eyes and say something, anything. Father doesn't stop squeezing her hand and I don't let go of her other one. No one is shedding any tears; it's just trying to come to terms with the sudden finality. The words that doctor Kuzi has said stick to my head, that mother must have felt at peace enough to let go. Mother has passed on with the knowledge that at last she has seen her two boys again; they look healthy and they are going to look after their father. I surmise that in her heart she must have felt the peace that had eluded her for twenty – one years. Life can really be cruel, I am thinking as I look over at father and Chris, who has now let go of father's shoulder and mother's hand and is standing there just looking at mother's face. He notices me looking at him and walks around the bed as I let go of mother's left hand, stand up as Scarlett moves back a little and Chris moves forward and we embrace in a really tight hug. Scarlett moves back and allows us to share this moment, and she gently walks over to where father is still holding mother's right hand and she places her left hand on his shoulders, rubbing his right arm as she does so, with her right hand. It feels so surreal. A while back I did not know anything about my birth parents being alive, I did not know that I had a brother, let alone a twin at that, and now, after the roller – coaster of events that have taken place, we have all been reunited and now fate has conspired to take mother away.

People often say that things like these are expected and we knew that it would happen at any given time but it still hurts. I feel that we have been robbed of the chance to get to know mother a little bit more, even though we had shared all the stories of our lives, as much as we could with her between her rests. She had been moved to tears upon hearing of Chris's story but amazingly, Chris had assured her that his upbringing had never eroded the values that he had been born with, values encoded in his DNA passed on to him by mother. That had moved her even more to tears but Chris had been very reassuring, and I had felt so proud of him and wished that we had been together growing up, he seems like the kind of big brother who could take care of everything and put everyone at ease. One thing that had stood out is a quote that Chris had mentioned whilst holding mother's hand not more than a few hours ago, as I recall. He had told mother that he had read somewhere that resilience is not about avoiding adversity; it's about facing it head – on and emerging stronger than before. That had really hit me, and the admiration for Chris had gone up a notch. I wonder if that had been me, would I have been behaving the way that Chris is, not feeling bitter and taking everything as it comes. Chris had obviously been taught in the school of hard knocks and had emerged from it wise and proper.

Father eventually sits down as does Scarlet. He bows his head as we all do and he starts saying a prayer, thanking God for mother and the joy, wisdom, stability and reason that she had brought to this world, and for always being his rock in all the times of adversity that they had faced, without complaining even once, without laying the blame on any one else whatsoever. He gives thanks that The Lord has allowed her final wish to come true; the wish that she had fervently prayed for even before that dreaded cancer had invaded her body. That one day, even on her death bed, she would be able to see her two sons and be able to hold their hands in hers and to tell them how much she loved them. To tell them that not a single day had passed by that she had not said a prayer for them, asking The Almighty to guide their every step, to show them how to love, to have respect for humankind, to show integrity and on top of all, how she had prayed to The Lord to give them kind, giving hearts, as it costs nothing to be kind. At this time, I am in tears, I cannot hold it in. Chris reaches out and takes my left hand in his right and I look at him and he is shedding tears too. Eventually there is not a dry tear in here and finally father has finished praying. He says "amen" and we join him in saying "The Grace" and we all conclude with "Amen".

Mother looks so peaceful, even in death.

CHAPTER FORTY-SEVEN

The funeral is taking place at the hospice where mother had designated a place for her to be laid to rest. Mother had apparently instructed father that she did not want to be cremated, she had wanted to have a memorial site where her two sons could come and spend time with her, and it feels as if she knew what she had planned the way that things had panned out. Mother is going to be laid to rest in the grounds where Chris and I have met her and also said our goodbyes albeit not in the usual way.

Mother had said that she had not wanted her funeral to be a big occasion, just a short celebration of her life with the people that she loved and were dear to her. The hospice has a chaplain who is in charge of the funeral ceremony and we are gathered in mother's final resting place. There are not many of us, just as mother would have wanted. There's father, Chris, Scarlett, Allegra and Aurelia, Alex and his family, Samuel, who is walking gingerly with the aid of clutches, Brenda, Sheila, the housekeeping staff, a few of father's and mother's employees form CODENEINNIS, Martin, and a few of other employees at the mansion, doctor Kuzi and some of her staff and the hospice chaplain, and myself.

Everyone is wearing black; it is a cool cloudy day with the hint of showers but the heat has somehow dissipated. Mother had insisted on being buried in a normal coffin; she did not want father spending a fortune that could be spent on a needy cause. That was mother to the end, father had lamented. The chaplain leads the ceremony by intoning a prayer and reads a few verses from the Bible, then offers a short reflection of the selfless life that mother has lived. The coffin stands ready, waiting to be lowered into the grave. The pallbearers have included father, Chris, Alex, Martin, myself and some of the housekeeping male staff. The coffin is then lowered into the earth using a lowering device as we all stand and witness this final stage of the service.

Father, Chris and I are asked to scatter soil in the grave and after we have done this everyone else follows suit. The grave is then covered to the full with soil and I realise that this is done by the grounds keeping staff and Chris opts to help and as he does so, I ask for a shovel and lend a helping hand too. Chris and I are asked to plant the white wooden cross on top of the grave, the cross bearing the message that herein lies Kathleen Keynudhia, wife and mother; and denotes the date of birth and the date of her passing. We all then place lovely looking flowers and at the end, you can hardly see the soil because of the amazing array of flowers atop the grave. After most of the mourners have left, father, Chris, Scarlett, Allegra, Aurelia and I remain at the gravesite for a while longer. We are holding hands and as father leads us into a solemn thanksgiving prayer as the heavens open and light rain begins to fall. We make our way back inside the hospice where the hospice team are gathered, offering good wishes and condolences to father and his family.

Father thanks every one of the staff and we walk to the car park where there are most of his employees gathered, each shaking his and our hands and finally everyone is driven off or drives off. The journey back to the house is done in silence and as soon as we get inside only Chris and I are sat in one of the living rooms, and we chat about mundane things like life in England, sports and hobbies. I realise that we are avoiding talking about what has happened, which suits me fine.

Acknowledgement

Writing Broken Glass has been a journey of reflection, discovery, and healing one I could not have completed alone.

First and foremost, I want to thank those who have walked beside me in life, knowingly or unknowingly shaping the thoughts that found their way onto these pages. To the quiet listeners, the patient friends, and the fierce believers — your presence made all the difference.

To my editor and publishing team, thank you for your insight, guidance, and care in bringing this story to life. Your commitment to detail and respect for the narrative made this process far more rewarding than I could have imagined.

To the readers — those who pick up this book with open minds and open hearts — thank you. It is for you that this story was told.

Lastly, to the unseen stories, the silent struggles, and the broken pieces we all carry — this book is a tribute.

With gratitude,

Epilogue

The mood and the atmosphere in the formal dining room is of calmness and joy. As I look around the room, I realise that there is no other place that I would rather be at this very moment in time but here. People are sitting and others are standing. Father is busy at the far end of the table with two of his senior vice presidents, Allegra and Aurelia are in what appears to be an animated conversation with Scarlett, Jasmine and Maxine. Samuel, Chris and surprisingly, Jorum, who father got picked up from the airport yesterday, and the happiest person had been Chris to see him, are discussing something and Alex is sitting next to me, as usual sipping his Macallan with ice and he appears to be a content man.

I am feeling at home, and it is three days since mother's funeral. Father had explained to us that he and mother are the ones that had broken a family tradition; mother had been an only child; her mother had passed away before her father followed her a few years later. Father had thought that he was the only child to his mother until he had found out about Marcus, which is the reason why he had wanted to help him in the first place. By breaking the family tradition, father had explained that they are the ones who had more than one child, and had explained that it was a blessing from above. Yesterday, after this huge guy Jorum had been picked up from the airport, father had him seen to by a doctor and he had appeared very grateful. Father had called Chris, Scarlett and I in his study where we had discussed the way forward.

Father had reiterated that Chris and I were now the sole owners of the company with the backing of his full team, and that he would still remain on in an advisory role, which Chris and I have appreciated.

Father had reminded Scarlett and I that because we still had our jobs back in England (with all that had been going on we had forgotten that we only had a few days of annual leave left), the best thing was to let us make our own decisions, he would wait for whatever I decided. I had spoken to my adoptive parents in England and had filled them in on everything. They had been saddened at mother's death but had understood. Alex had knocked on the door at some point and had spent time to update us on Francis, who had completely slipped my mind with all the goings – on. He intimated that Francis had made a full recovery and he and Mr Atkins were forming a law partnership and the first person that they were going to go after was, no surprises, Marcus. At this news, father had looked at Chris and winked at him and had mouthed the words "comeuppance, son, comeuppance".

I had asked about the dead man that I had been arrested for, and Alex had explained that it had been a ruse by Marcus; he had told one of his low – life drug peddlers to pass information that it had been Chris who had carried out a murder that had been in a cold case file for just four years, with the hope of Chris being picked up so that Marcus could get his hands on him. Chris at this time had been hiding out at his disused warehouse, Marcus knew where I lived; but could never show his hand at trying to grab because he was aware of the protection accorded me which I had no idea about, it had been that easy but there had not been a shred of evidence. The so – called informer had allegedly been charged with wasting police time.

Apparently the two men who had been at the magistrate's court had not been sent by Marcus; their aim had been to seize me thinking that I was Chris and use me as a bargaining chip with Marcus as he had double – crossed them on a drug deal. They had been part of Marcus's Street crew and had been informed of how important Chris was to Marcus. They had not wanted to abduct me in the vicinity of the magistrate's court; they were both heroin addicts who could not think for themselves. Allegedly they had been told that Boris, the driver, would pick Francis and Chris up and take them to Marcus but that had not gone to plan. Francis had realised this somehow after he had been shot and had done what he had done in a valiant effort to save who he thought was Chris's life. The two men had tried to get away but had been arrested by the police but had not given Marcus up, it seems that their drug induced brains had not wanted to rat on one of their low life's.

Francis had told the police that the men had approached he and Chris and demanded that Chris be handed over to them, and Francis had made a mental calculation to get away from what he had perceived as danger.

Father has announced that once he has fully recovered, Samuel is welcome to work in his company with his accounting skills. Jorum has agreed to undergo training, once he recuperates, to join father's security team, he has been impressed by what he has seen. Alex and his wife have been offered the chance to join the company as well, he has said that he and Maxine will think about it. The sisters will be going back to university soon, as is Jasmine, who is eager to come back to this place as long as we can invite her, which Chris assures her that is not a problem. Scarlett and I have both sent emails and written resignation letters to our respective hospital trusts. We hope that they will understand. Father has invited Scarlett's parents over and has told them over several video calls that they are more than welcome to stay for as long as they want to in his home. Father has then stated that this weekend there will be an official welcoming home party, and everybody better get ready to have some fun. Father, Chris, and I stand on the lush, green, well-manicured lawn, looking out to the impressive blue Indian Ocean with the cool evening breeze blowing, and the world, even though devoid of mother, feels quite content. Chris and I are both wearing matching brown beach shorts, orange loose short-sleeved t – t-shirts and brown sandals as we stand either side of father, who has a glass of water in his right hand. He is wearing grey trousers, a blue shirt with all kinds of rose flowers on it, brown sandals and is staring out to the ocean just like Chris and I. Chris and I have decided to change our names to James and Joshua as a final tribute to mother, and father has been overjoyed by this news. From then henceforth, we are going to be known as James and Joshua Keynudhia, and it sounds just right.

The others are all in the house; they understand that this is an important time for a father to share some moments with his sons.

Father turns to each of us, looks deep in the eye, and says, "Remember this wherever you go. Glass, once shattered, even if you manage to somehow put it back together, remains broken, but the pieces can be picked up and glued together to form some semblance of normality."

We all embrace in a group hug as the sun starts to sink over the horizon, over the blue shimmering waters of the beautiful, majestic Indian Ocean.

A disco ball is made from hundreds of pieces of broken glass – yet together, they create something dazzling and full of light. You are not broken. You're a disco ball. Keep shining...

www.ingramcontent.com/pod-product-compliance
Lightning Source LLC
Chambersburg PA
CBHW050405260626
47156CB00003B/883